Summer Sunrise CONFIDENTIAL

by Melissa J. Morgan

Grosset & Dunlap

GROSSET & DUNLAP
Published by the Penguin Group
Penguin Group (USA) Inc., 375 Hudson Street, New York, New York 10014, USA
Penguin Group (Canada), 90 Eglinton Avenue East, Suite 700,
Toronto, Ontario M4P 2Y3, Canada
(a division of Pearson Penguin Canada Inc.)
Penguin Books Ltd., 80 Strand, London WC2R 0RL, England
Penguin Group Ireland, 25 St. Stephen's Green, Dublin 2, Ireland
(a division of Penguin Books Ltd.)
Penguin Group (Australia), 250 Camberwell Road, Camberwell, Victoria 3124, Australia
(a division of Pearson Australia Group Pty. Ltd.)
Penguin Books India Pvt. Ltd., 11 Community Centre, Panchsheel Park,
New Delhi—110 017, India
Penguin Group (NZ), 67 Apollo Drive, Rosedale, North Shore 0632, New Zealand
(a division of Pearson New Zealand Ltd.)
Penguin Books (South Africa) (Pty.) Ltd., 24 Sturdee Avenue,
Rosebank, Johannesburg 2196, South Africa

Penguin Books Ltd., Registered Offices:
80 Strand, London WC2R 0RL, England

Text copyright © 2009 by Grosset & Dunlap. All rights reserved. Published by Grosset & Dunlap,
a division of Penguin Young Readers Group, 345 Hudson Street, New York, New York 10014.
GROSSET & DUNLAP is a trademark of Penguin Group (USA) Inc. Printed in the U.S.A.

Library of Congress Control Number: 2008023047

ISBN 978-0-448-44988-3   10 9 8 7 6 5 4 3 2 1

One

Cassie Hamilton wasn't exactly the type of girl to go to summer camp. She didn't know how to pitch a tent. She could live her whole life without braving bug juice. She had absolutely no desire to capture anyone's flag. She just wasn't a joiner, and yet here she was—joining the crowd on the beach campus of Camp Ohana, a water-sports camp in her hometown of Kalui Kona, Hawaii. Cassie knew that Ohana wasn't a typical summer camp, and that's why she was here—but with all the shrieking, singing, and chanting (yes, *chanting*) coming from the excited campers on the beach, it sure sounded like one.

"*O* to the *H* to the *A* to the *Naaaaa*!" The campers were chanting this with such ferocious enthusiasm that Cassie felt like she'd stepped into some kind of cult revival. If she wasn't so determined to do something different with herself this summer, she might have turned around and gone home.

Then again, she wasn't actually *going* to summer camp. She was sixteen, too old to be an actual camper. She was here to be a C.I.T., a counselor-in-training. That meant she'd have to help the counselors and junior counselors organize these overenthusiastic campers. She'd have to find a way to calm the kids down long enough to take a dip in the water without giving the ocean a seizure. Talk about madness.

She was here, but that didn't mean she had any idea where to go. Then she noticed a hand-painted banner hanging between two palm trees. ALOHA, C.I.T.S!! SIGN IN HERE!!! it said in turquoise letters with pink flowers dotting the *I*'s. She headed straight for it. The C.I.T. program director—her lei nametag said Simona—was sitting at a small table under the banner. She was busy signing in another girl, so Cassie waited patiently for her turn. She put down her backpack. Shoved her banana-yellow surfboard in the sand. Closed her eyes. Breathed in the scent of the island—a mix of tropical flowers, salt water, and cool volcanic wind, like no other place in the world. Listened for the waves. Felt the warm sand bury her toes. Took a long moment.

This was her home; she was born and raised in Kona on Big Island. Even so, she wasn't on the island so much anymore. Cassie had turned pro as a surfer more than four years ago, and since then she'd traveled to most beaches worth surfing, from Oahu to California to Australia to Japan and beyond. Usually her summers—all year, really—were about training and competing and, hopefully, winning. It was weird to be staying in one place for a whole summer.

That was how Cassie felt right now . . . weird. Out of sorts. She wasn't herself. Ever since the—

Suddenly Cassie heard whispering nearby. She probably wouldn't have even noticed, except it seemed to be about her.

"She is *not* a C.I.T."

"She is so."

"Nooooo waaaaay. That's crazy. Don't you think she has better things to do?"

"What, she's just chilling out here for no reason?"

"I'm telling you, there is *no way*. Pros don't take

the summer off to work at a sleepaway camp. That's insane. That's like Scarlett Johansson giving up her Oscar to work at the Gap."

"Scarlett Johansson never got an Oscar."

"You know what I mean."

"I bet you I'm right. I bet you a soda from the canteen, any flavor you want."

Cassie was clearly being paranoid. They weren't betting *soda* on the fact that she was here as a C.I.T. . . . were they?

Cassie turned to look. Two girls her age were on the sand nearby, openly staring at her. When Cassie stared back, the girl with the dark hair quickly averted her eyes. But the other girl—she had pale blond hair and a tan so even it looked artificial—she met Cassie's eyes, unflinching. They must have signed in already, because they wore their C.I.T. nametag leis. The girl with the dark hair was Emmy. The other was Danica.

So what if they knew who she was? Cassie smiled, acting like she hadn't heard them. Both girls returned her smile. Now it was all smiles and sunshine, sunshine and smiles, everyone hap-hap-happy except Cassie, who was trying not to squirm in her flip-flops. She'd figured some people would recognize her here—she'd visited Ohana a year before to do a surfing exposition. But she didn't expect it to feel like this. So *exposed*.

"Hey there, are you here to sign in?" called Simona.

"Yeah," Cassie said enthusiastically. She stepped up to the table so Simona could hand her the lei with her name on it, but Simona was taking her time searching through all the leis, like she was having trouble finding Cassie's.

Cassie's smile faltered when she noticed Simona pass over the lei that said *Cassie* and keep digging. *Wait . . . she doesn't recognize me?* Cassie thought.

Simona dropped the leis and leaned forward over the small table—made smaller by the fact that Simona was a very, very big girl. *Imposing* was the word. Cassie had competed against some killer surfer girls out on the junior circuit, but if she'd met Simona on the water, she would have been intimidated to fight her for any wave. "Just remind me of your name," Simona said at last. "You're a C.I.T., right? Let's make sure we've got you on the list."

Oh, Cassie realized. *She really actually doesn't know who I am.*

Cassie felt funny about that. On the one hand, two girls who knew exactly who Cassie was were ragging on her about being here. On the other, the person in charge of the C.I.T.s had no clue who she was. Cassie was surprised to find herself torn between the two reactions, not sure which was worse.

Not that Cassie was into fame and celebrity and autographing surfboards or any of that—though she had autographed a few surfboards, just like any pro. If you surfed a good run, if you won a contest or two and were good enough to get a sponsor like Coco Beach, Cassie's sponsor, you'd get your photo in a surf magazine and people started to know who you were. It's not like Cassie got mobbed at airports. Still, she realized, she actually *liked* the comfort of familiarity. And of all people, she'd felt sure Simona would know who she was.

"Cassie Hamilton," Cassie said.

Simona pulled out the pink lei with Cassie's name pinned to it. "Remind me, are you here as a regular C.I.T. assigned to one of the bunks, or as a specialty C.I.T.?"

"Specialty," Cassie said. Her voice was more quiet than usual. She dropped the lei around her neck.

Simona noticed the yellow surfboard stuck in the sand behind Cassie. "Not the surfing C.I.T., though," Simona said, seeming confused. "I hope there wasn't any miscommunication about this. I thought I already signed in the surfing C.I.T. Sorry, so many names today. Danica!" she yelled suddenly.

Danica—the blonde who'd been giving Cassie the stink-eye before—sauntered over.

"Danica, there aren't two girls' surfing C.I.T.s this year, are there?" Simona asked. "If so, the counselors should have really told me."

"Not that I know of," Danica said in a sharp voice.

Simona turned to Cassie. "Danica's been coming to Ohana since she was . . . Danica, how old were you when you first came here?"

"Nine," Danica said. "I've been coming here every summer since forever, so I know Ohana better than anyone, obviously. This is the first year I'll be a C.I.T., and I'm *so excited.*" She smiled wide, and Simona beamed at her. She was clearly a favorite.

"*Danica's* the surfing C.I.T.," Simona said slowly. She took another look at Cassie's bright yellow board—impossible to miss in the brilliant sun—and added, "Cassie, I hope you didn't think—"

"No, I didn't, really," Cassie said, interrupting her awkwardly. "I mean I know I'm not the surfing C.I.T., I mean, I *was*, I mean that's why I applied. But then I changed my mind."

Danica's face got very pinched at this admission. Maybe she thought she'd been the surfing counselors' first choice.

"I'm here to help the swimming counselors," Cassie said. She shrugged, realizing how odd that might seem to anyone who knew she surfed pro.

Originally, when Cassie had applied to be a counselor-in-training at Camp Ohana, she'd signed up to coach the kids with surfing lessons. She thought it would be no problem. Then—and she couldn't explain this to her parents or her friends and especially not to her surfing coach—she realized she couldn't do it. She just couldn't. So she changed her mind. Being the swimming C.I.T. was the best choice for her this summer: She could be here, taking the summer off like she wanted, without pressure to surf.

Simona seemed relieved that there was no confusion over C.I.T. assignments. "Well, if there are any other questions, we'll get them sorted out at orientation," she said. "Cassie, you met Danica. And that's Emmy. She's one of our lifeguards. Listen, I've got to run for just two seconds. Danica, if any new C.I.T.s come by, could you sign them in? And could you point Cassie in the direction of the C.I.T. bunk?" And then Simona was bounding off toward the crowd of screamers, bleating on a whistle.

"It's, uh, great to meet you guys," Cassie said.

"Nice board," Danica said, taking Simona's seat behind the table.

"Thanks," Cassie said.

"Too bad you won't have so much time to, you know, *surf* on it," Danica said. "They keep the C.I.T.s, like, superbusy."

"Do they?" Cassie said. She was happy to hear it.

Danica nodded solemnly. "Waiting tables, doing dishes, garbage runs, scrubbing the showers, cleaning trash off the beach—you know, the grunt work."

"She's exaggerating," Emmy said. "It's not all work. Like tonight—"

Danica cut her off. "I'm dying of thirst." She set her eyes on Emmy. "I want a soda. Could you grab me one at the canteen?"

"Yeah, sure," Emmy said. She headed off down the sand.

Now Cassie was alone with Danica. She wondered if Danica would ask her about the surfing C.I.T. position, like what happened, and why she changed her mind. But Danica did no such thing. "The C.I.T. bunk's that way," she said. She pointed a tanned arm, her finger aimed lazily at the cluster of small buildings in the distance, impossible to tell which one. It was the most unhelpful kind of directions she could have given.

But all Cassie said was: "Thanks. See you later!" Something about this girl put her on edge.

Cassie lugged her backpack onto her shoulders, balanced her surfboard over her head, and set off. The path looked like an obstacle course. Between where Cassie stood on the sand and the colorful makeshift buildings in the distance were too many things and people to leap over, duck under, and dive past. It would take Cassie a year and a day to find the C.I.T. bunk. So she decided on a detour. She kicked off her flip-flops and stuck her bare feet in the sand. She dropped her backpack, dropped her board. She found herself getting closer and closer to the shoreline, until her toes were good and buried in the tide and she wasn't so much walking as standing there, looking out at the water, like she had nowhere else to be.

Figures. Even though Cassie hadn't set foot on a surfboard in months, she still was most comfortable beside the ocean. It felt like it belonged to her, that she belonged in it. How it could also be the thing she was most afraid of made absolutely no sense.

"Cassie! Cassie! Cassie!" she heard in the distance.

And then there—running straight at her like a blond-tressed linebacker all suited up in the latest Marc Jacobs (which made no sense really, a football player in Marc Jacobs, but that's how it was)—was the one person at camp this summer who knew exactly who she was. This girl would never judge her. This was Cassie's younger cousin, Tori, who was spending the summer at Ohana, too. Cassie had been the one to tell Tori about the camp. Tori used to go to a summer camp on the mainland in Pennsylvania, but it had closed down. In a way, they were both starting anew this summer.

"Cass, where have you *been*?" Tori was saying. "I've been looking *everywhere*!" Then she flung her arms around Cassie, almost knocking them both in the ocean.

Tori was an L.A. girl, born and bred, which meant she was always one step ahead when it came to fashion—and pretty much everything else, too. She was fourteen, two years younger than Cassie, so she was here as a camper, but you wouldn't know that from meeting her. She acted sixteen, at least. Sometimes Cassie felt like the younger one.

Tori broke out of the hug and stared at Cassie intently. "You're moping," Tori said. She gave Cassie a mock-serious look. "Cass! It's the first day of camp and you're being a big mope. Stop it!"

"I'm not, I swear," Cassie said, trying to deny it.

"Cass, no one *knows*," Tori said. "It's not like with your other friends, how all they do is go surfing or talk about going surfing or listen to the weather report to see if it's time to go surfing. Seriously, there are tons of other things going on here. This is *camp*."

"I think people do know," Cassie said. "There were some girls . . . they were talking about me."

"What girls, where?" Tori asked. She spun around on the sand wildly, as if to prove her point. "You are completely and totally paranoid!"

Cassie tried to describe them. "Other C.I.T.s. They were both really pretty. One was Hawaiian, I think she was the lifeguard. And the other had this long blond hair, real tan, she had on a white bikini . . ."

"Oh, Emmy and Danica," Tori said.

"You know them already? How—?"

Tori just smiled, shrugging helplessly. "I just, I don't know, met them or whatever."

"God, Tor, you know everyone, and you've only been here five minutes."

"I highly doubt they were saying anything bad about you. Maybe they just liked your . . ." She paused, checking out Cassie's outfit, which consisted of a sleeveless surfing shirt, boardies, and plain turquoise flip-flops. "Your flip-flops? Anyway, I promise you, Cass, no one knows about the accid—" Tori began, but before she could even finish her sentence, Cassie had jammed her hand over her cousin's mouth.

17

"Could we maybe not talk about it?" Cassie said.

Tori carefully removed Cassie's hand from her mouth. Then she pantomimed zipping her lips closed. Then, to keep the charade going, she mimed swimming out into the ocean, and doing a hula dance, or the moonwalk maybe, it was hard to tell what Tori was trying to communicate except that she was being a huge goof-off. Whenever they were together, things got a little childish. Probably it was genetic.

"*What* are you doing, Tor?" Cassie said, bursting out laughing.

"Cheering you up. And guess what? It worked. C'mon, let's get your stuff to the bunk and then I'll introduce you around."

"You'll introduce *me*? I'm the C.I.T., you're just a camper!"

"That's my great talent," Tori said, "making friends. Your talent is surfing"—catching the look on Cassie's face, she added—"and moping. You have a great talent for moping! C'mon, Cass, let's go."

Cassie took one last glance at the ocean. She could have been training for pipelines right now.

Instead she was here. She grabbed her backpack, propped her brand-new board on her head, and followed her cousin to her new summer home. This was Camp Ohana—*ohana* meant "family" in Hawaiian.

We'll see about that, Cassie thought.

Tori sure knew her way around the campgrounds. Without a second thought, she led Cassie straight for a pebble-strewn path near a stand of palm trees. Stuck in the sand was a signpost with arrows pointing this way and that. Each arrow was a different color, with symbols of animals carved on each one. The whole effect was much like stumbling upon a village of some hidden civilization deep in the middle of a rain forest. On the arrows, Cassie noticed a dolphin, a bird, some kind of pointy-finned fish . . . before Tori let out a yelp and pulled her down a fork in the path. "Hey, Tasha, hey, Carlie. Hi, Bobby! Jana, what's up?" Tori chattered to different campers as they went.

Suddenly, Tori came to a stop. "Okay, I'm in that one over there, bunk G-14," she said, pointing to a small bunk with a stunning bright green door. "The *pinao* bunk, whatever that means."

"Dragonfly," Cassie said—finally she knew something Tori didn't! "*Pinao* means 'dragonfly' in Hawaiian."

"Cool," Tori said. "Looks like all the bunks have Hawaiian names, because I think you're in that one." She pointed to a bunk with a turquoise door. A faded and peeling *G-16* was painted on it. A small lanai—or porch—wrapped around the front, and painted at the top was the name of the bunk: *nai'a*. In Hawaiian that meant "dolphin."

A girl was coming down the stairs, an orange C.I.T. lei around her neck. Her wavy auburn hair frizzed out from the heat, but she didn't seem to care. She had bright pink cheeks, intensely friendly blue-green eyes, and was filled with so much energy she seemed like she might pop. She bounded over to Tori and Cassie and quickly bleated, "Aloha, aloha, I'm Andi. Can't wait to meet you guys later, bye!" And with that she was down the pebbled path, heading for the beach.

"Um, wow," Cassie said. "She seems nice."

"Totally," Tori said. "See? You met someone

already. And check out these hammocks." A few hammocks were strung up in the trees. Maybe, on a hot night, if the bunk was too stuffy, C.I.T.s could sleep out there. "Besides," Tori continued, "I have something that'll make you stop moping. Your birthday present!"

"My . . . *birthday* present?" Cassie said. Her birthday was, what? Five months ago. But there was no time to protest, as Tori was now pulling Cassie into the bunk, where they found themselves blissfully alone.

"Where is everybody?" Cassie said.

"I guess they're all out being C.I.T.s or whatever," Tori said. "So I'll be quick. I meant to send this to you months ago, I swear! I just totally blanked. I'm a sucky cousin. Can you ever forgive me?"

Tori looked so serious, her blue-green eyes wide, her forehead all wrinkled up like she'd shoved a leg of pantyhose over her face so she could rob a convenience store. She was too much. "Tori, don't worry about it," Cassie said. "We live, like, thousands of miles apart. Besides, I didn't get you a birthday present either, did I?"

Tori dropped her eyes to her Alice & Olivia

platform sandals—not exactly practical, the heels sunk into the sand. "Uh, yeah, you got me a DVD," she admitted. "The latest *Pirates of the Caribbean*. You always know how I feel about Orlando." She sighed. Then she looked up, eyes bright again. *"But I am so glad we're alone right now because I am so going to make it up to you, so just open this!"* From her Balenciaga shoulder bag she pulled out a puffy present wrapped in what looked like a glossy jungle of lipsticked mouths and painted eyes. Lots and lots of mouths and eyes.

"What is that?" Cassie said. It looked either sexy and cool, or semi-deformed.

"Wrapping paper," Tori said with a shrug. "I took scissors to Italian *Vogue*. Just *open it*! Before someone comes in!"

Cassie opened the present to reveal the most intensely shiny, blindingly bright object she had ever seen in her life, apart from the sun.

"Do you love it, or do you love it!" Tori shrieked.

"I . . ." Cassie stretched it out to get the full effect—it was made of spandex, it was . . . *Oh no, oh yes, oh* god, *it's a bathing suit*, she realized. It was a gold one-piece with gigantic slits up the sides and a neckline that plunged so far down, it was nearly impossible to tell the back from the front. "I'm, what's the word? Speechless," Cassie said at last. She wasn't sure how the suit would stay on.

"*Exactly*. That was my *exact* reaction when I saw it at the boutique. It's Dolce & Gabbana, you know. It's so delicious, don't you just want to eat it?"

In fact, Cassie would probably *eat* the gold bathing suit before she'd wear it out in actual water, now that Tori said it. But her cousin meant well. This was just like Tori—she was fabulous, even at fourteen years old. Cassie figured she just couldn't help it. Maybe it was anthropologically impossible to grow up within a ten-mile radius of Hollywood without having at least some glamour rub off on you. But just because Tori was fabulous didn't mean she was a snob about people who weren't. She wanted to share. She'd share her hundred-dollar lip gloss with you just as soon as she'd share her peanuts if you happened to sit next to her on an airplane.

The thing is, maybe Tori could pull off a gold D&G "bathing suit"—but Cassie sure couldn't.

Cassie wore *surfer* bathing suits. As in suits

with bottoms that looked more like shorts. Suits with tops that actually stayed on when the waves came splashing. She'd be stripped naked in two seconds flat if she went out on her board in that suit.

But she loved her cousin, so she tried to pull the shock off her face and smile. She just hoped Tori didn't ask her to try it on.

Too late. "Put it on! Put it on! Put it on!" Tori was chanting like the camp-happy kids out in the sand. "Cass, you have to. Pleeeeeeeeeaaase?" She stuck out her lower lip.

"Okay already! But Tor . . . I don't know if I can pull this off."

Tori shook her head, hotly denying it. "You can so pull it off. All that surfing? Look at your bod." She turned Cassie to face a floor-length mirror beside the entry to the bathroom. "You are hot," she whispered in Cassie's ear. "Go change into that suit, hottie. I'll pick out a bed for you while you do."

Cassie stepped into a bathroom stall to put the gold contraption on. She was glad no one could see her because at first she put her leg through the arm hole and had the suit on all crooked. Finally she pulled the straps up and got the gold pieces of

24

spandex covering what they were made to cover, and she went back into the bunk.

Meanwhile, Tori had put Cassie's backpack on a bed close to a window. "In my bunk we have bunk beds, but I guess you C.I.T.s are too mature for that—oh." She'd caught sight of Cassie and stopped talking.

Cassie covered herself with her hands. "Is it that bad?"

Of course it's that bad. Only a Victoria's Secret model could pull this off!

But Tori was shaking her head and smiling. "You look really good, Cass, I'm serious. This is, like, the best birthday present I've ever gotten anyone, like, ever. I should get an award for this. Or a write-up in *Vogue* or something."

"You are *crazy*," Cassie repeated. "C-R-A-Z—" But before she made it to *Y*, she caught a glimpse of her reflection in the grimy camp mirror. Through the dirty haze covering the glass—smeared with, what was that, Vaseline?—she saw herself in the D&G suit. And she looked pretty good if she did say so herself. Some might say hot, even. It was surreal.

"Walk for me," Tori said. "Just to your bed and back. I need the full effect."

25

In the gold suit Cassie felt like another person. She wasn't the serious surfer girl who thought only about her next competition. And she wasn't the girl who came after, after the incident that made her stop surfing, the one who didn't want to get back on the board. She was something else entirely.

It was this other Cassie who walked down the aisle between the beds like a model.

Tori was clapping and stomping her feet and shouting for more. And Cassie was giving it to her, a swish here, a swish there, a turn, a pose with hip out, a pose with arms up, another swish, another turn, a—

Oh.

God.

Please.

No.

Cassie had reached the end of her fantasy runway and was now facing the worst possible sight a girl in a Glamazon bathing suit could imagine in her deepest, most mortifying nightmares: not just another human being, but a boy human being. A very, very gorgeous boy.

Cassie, seeing as she was standing there half naked, let out a shriek and dove behind the closest bed. Tori shot forward and tried to block her from sight. And Gorgeous Boy himself? He stood there frozen like he'd just caught sight of a UFO. The door to the bunk slammed shut in its frame.

It was a deathly long series of moments before anyone could find the voice to speak, followed by all three speaking at the exact same moment.

"Don't you know how to knock?" said Tori.

"This is not what it looks like," said Cassie.

"I think maybe I'm in the wrong bunk," said Gorgeous Boy.

Cassie couldn't look at him. So she looked instead at his feet. He had nice feet. Thankfully her cousin took hold of the conversation for her.

"Dude," Tori answered him. "The wrong bunk, hello, you *think*?"

"I'm Micah, by the way," he said. "And isn't this B-16? On the door it said . . ."

"I'm telling you, this is definitely not a boys' bunk," Tori said.

"But it says right here . . ." Micah said. He pulled out a piece of paper.

Tori grabbed it to prove her point. "You're in the hummahummahumma, um, I-can't-pronounce-it bunk. It says right here."

Cassie knew without having to see the paper. If all bunks were given the names of Hawaiian animals, birds, and fish, the name of his bunk would have to be the *humuhumunukunukuapua'a* bunk. That was the actual, practically-impossible-to-pronounce name for the Hawaii state fish.

"This is the *nai'a* bunk," she said. "Besides, this is G-16, not B-16. It's sort of hard to read on the door."

He laughed. "Yeah. I guess so."

Cassie realized she was still hiding behind a bed. She tried to stand up. She looked for the first time at his face. He had dark hair, curling near his ears, and warm brown eyes, and cocoa-colored skin. His face was, well, even better-looking than his feet.

"I, uh, like your suit," he said. His eye twitched.

Was that a wink?! He wasn't trying to WINK at me, was he?

No. No, he was just looking a bit embarrassed. "Guess I'll go find the right bunk then." He lifted his bag over his shoulder, then turned back to Cassie. "I'm really sorry I barged in on you when you were, um, you know."

28

"Me too," Cassie said.

He looked away then, opened the door, and stepped out.

Once the door slammed shut, Cassie keeled over onto the closest bed. She shouted something into the mattress. "Mmm ggggiiiing t' dieeeeee."

"What?" Tori said softly, sitting beside her.

With great effort, Cassie lifted her head. She had been so sure of herself for a second there, but it was gone now, all gone. "I said: I am going to die."

Tori, on the other hand, was smiling. "What are you talking about, Cass? That was the best thing that could have happened. What luck!"

"Luck! Luck? Tori, he just saw me in this, in this, I'm sorry, Tor, but this hella awful suit, he *saw me.* Like what could possibly be worse than that?"

Tori gave a little pout at Cassie calling her birthday gift "hella awful," but she still had that insane smile on her face. "You're looking at this all wrong. One of the hottest guys here just saw you looking killer in an unforgettable bathing suit. That is what I call a perfect bit of luck. And it's all thanks to me." She winked. "I say you owe me, big time."

TWO

Micah Sims wanted to shove his head in the sand—that's how stupid he felt for walking in on Cassie and that other girl doing whatever they were doing with that bathing suit. Actually, he didn't want to know what they were doing. Better not to know. He wanted to block the entire experience from memory, except maybe the quick glimpse he got of Cassie. Fact is, she looked hot.

Not that she didn't look hot normally . . .

But at that moment when he'd walked in . . .

Uh, yeah.

Micah was seriously relieved the girls couldn't read his mind.

Micah was well aware of who Cassie was—the gossip that she was inexplicably here for the summer had surely crossed the beach ten times by now.

Three separate people had told him. Besides, Micah remembered her from last summer, when he'd been at Ohana as a camper and Cassie had come with a group of surfers to do an exposition. It was hard to forget a girl like that: pretty, sure, and friendly, even though she was pro. Besides, from what he remembered when he saw her surfing, she had a killer cutback.

"Lost?" someone called to him.

Micah realized he was standing in the sand, looking like a dazed tourist.

"Micah, your bunk's over there—the one with the big *humuhumunukunukuapua'a* on it, you can't miss it. Gotta go! Simona's got me running to the—" And she didn't finish her sentence before bounding away down the path. He saw her auburn hair bouncing wildly behind her, and that was that.

Micah blinked. That was Andi, another C.I.T. She was so full of energy, it could be hard to take at times. Last summer, when they were both campers, he remembered her running around everywhere, doing fifteen things at once. Guess that hadn't changed. But she'd been right: He was standing outside his own bunk and didn't even realize it. The swimsuit incident had done more damage than he realized.

He dropped off his bag, claimed a bed, and then, just as he stepped out on the lanai, he ran into the one person he was hoping to avoid just a little longer: his girlfriend from last summer, Danica DeLaura.

He'd heard she was here, a C.I.T., too, but he was in a bit of denial about it. At the end of last summer she'd slipped him a note just before she got on the bus to the airport that basically said they were over. Not that they were so serious anyway, but still: a note? What was this, grade school?

"Micah," Danica said. It seemed like she'd been waiting for him outside the door. "We need to clear the air so let me go first." Micah noticed that she looked good, but then tried not to let her notice that he'd noticed. He'd have to play this game all summer now.

He leaned against the railing of the lanai and let her talk. Sure, she was the one to break up with him, but he wasn't about to give her the satisfaction of being a jerk.

"So," Danica said, "you're a surfing C.I.T. this summer, and I'm a surfing C.I.T., and since we'll have to work together, *obviously*, this isn't the time to—"

"Wait, you're the girls' surfing C.I.T.?" Micah said.

"Yeah," Danica said, her eyes narrowing. "Surprised?" She stood up straight, her shoulders back, all defensive.

"No, I just—"

"Micah, I know this'll be hard for you. The thing is"—and here her face softened and she changed the subject abruptly—"you look better than I remember you looking. What happened, you been working out?"

He wanted to roll his eyes. Instead he said, "I've been surfing. It's seriously all I've done since last summer."

"That's cute," she said. Then she added, sounding even more condescending, if that were possible, "You're not hoping to go pro, are you?"

Yeah, I am, he thought.

Something told him he shouldn't admit that to Danica, so he just shrugged, like he could go either way. Truth was, he'd been surfing nonstop all year. He lived in Waikui, so the waves were practically his backyard. It wasn't hard to get time in the water; what was hard was being taken seriously in a place where everyone had started surfing before they learned to walk. Though he'd lived in Hawaii for years, his family was originally from St. Louis, Missouri, far from any viable ocean. And the local surfers wouldn't let him forget it.

"You *do* want to go pro, don't you?" Danica purred, so sweet it was sickening. "And you think some sponsor'll notice you out here and invite you to some big fancy competition and you'll win it all. Oh, Micah . . ."

Micah just shrugged again. "Danica, what does this have to do with clearing the air, anyway? You're the one who gave me that stone-cold note."

"That note wasn't cold," Danica jumped in to say. "That note was *necessary*. I was the one who had the guts to say it first. I'm in Florida, you're in Waikui, what did you think would happen?! I was just being realistic."

"Yeah, I guess," he said. There was no point arguing it now.

Then she began talking again, something about how good he was looking—she just wouldn't let it go—and he would have been uncomfortable if the sight across the sand didn't distract him from whatever Danica was saying.

Two girls were stepping onto the lanai of the

girls' C.I.T. bunk: Cassie and the other girl who'd been with her. There was no trace of the gold bathing suit—Cassie was wearing the usual surfgirl uniform: boardies, a sleeveless rash guard, both pale blue. She had her hair pulled back in a ponytail. He tried not to make it obvious that he was watching her—he saw her walk down the steps, take the path toward the rec hall, not once looking in his direction. He tried not to show he was watching, but Danica caught him.

"Oh yeah, *her*," she said. "Can you believe her?"

"I think it's cool she's here as a C.I.T."

"Cool? It's pathetic. Something's up, something weird. That's what I think."

"What's weird is that she's not the girls' surfing C.I.T. and you are."

Danica gave him a look of death. "I've been coming to this camp since forever," she said. "The whole last year we were campers I worked on showing the counselors that I'm C.I.T. material. Clearly, they know I am. I deserve that spot. Besides, I applied for that surfing spot fair and square. *I'm* the surfing C.I.T. and she's not. She might have a name for herself out in the real world, but here she's a newbie. A nobody."

Micah smiled at Danica's tirade. "Sounds like someone's a little jealous."

"I am not dignifying that with an answer. Besides, I came here to talk about us, not that Cassie chick. We need to get this out of the way before orientation starts. Are you mature enough to handle working together this summer?"

"Are *you*?"

She stared, unblinking, into his eyes. Hers were a perfect shade of crystal clear green. Then, when he couldn't take his eyes off hers, she broke away and smiled a faint flirty smile. This was the Danica he remembered, the Danica he fell for last summer. "We'll see," she said.

Cassie was late to orientation, so late she pretty much missed the whole deal. She didn't know how it happened—she'd gone off to stow her surfboard somewhere, ran into Tori, met Tori's bunkmates, talked for a while, called her parents to say she'd settled in, took a walk by the water, maybe a longer walk than she'd meant to, and when she realized she was supposed to be at the C.I.T. and counselor orientation she was already an hour late. She ran across campus, but by the time she arrived she'd missed all the counselors' and junior counselors' names and hearing whatever assignment they all had for the evening.

In fact, the orientation was now breaking up and everyone was heading off as if they all had somewhere to be. Cassie followed some of the C.I.T.s toward what appeared to be the makings of a luau on the beach. She was relieved to find Tori sitting with her bunkmates near a small bonfire.

Cassie made her way over to her cousin. "Tor, I totally missed orientation," she confessed.

"What orientation?" Tori said.

"Exactly!" Cassie said.

"You should go tell someone," Tori said. "You should—"

Then a large shadow fell over the sand.

"Cassie," Simona said nicely enough—though so loud it broke up the girls' chatter, "aren't you one of my C.I.T.s? You're not here as a camper. The rest of the C.I.T.s are over there, making this luau happen." Then she walked away and left Cassie sitting there, her face hot and not because she was sitting so close to the fire.

"Oooooooh," said Tori's bunkmates in a hush.

Tori poked Cassie in the side. "Um, you should totally get up."

"Yeah," Cassie mumbled. She wasn't sure how she'd managed this one, but it looked like she was officially in trouble with the C.I.T. director on *her very first night at camp*. Cassie the surfer had been a trophy-winning phenom. Cassie the C.I.T. was turning out to be a bit of a mess.

"See you guys later," she said quickly to Tori's bunkmates and hustled over to the group of C.I.T.s that had gathered away from the bonfires.

"*Here* she is," Simona said as Cassie ran up. "As I was saying, the C.I.T.s have time for social hour later. Right now we're on the clock, and we want to make this a great first night for everyone. There's work to do, so hop to it!"

When the group scattered, Cassie rushed over to Simona. "I'm so, so sorry," Cassie said. "I got lost and missed orientation and—"

Simona held a hand up so she would stop talking. She gazed at Cassie for a long moment. "Some girls have wanted to be C.I.T.s for years," she said. "Not everyone who applies gets a position."

"Oh," Cassie said. She looked down at her feet. "I'm really sorry."

But Simona's face softened. "Just try not to miss anything else," she said. She waved Cassie toward the rest of the C.I.T.s, who had broken up into groups of three or four. Cassie noticed that the snobby C.I.T. from that morning, Danica, was with two girls who gave Cassie a shared stare-down as they passed on their way to the barbecues. Cassie looked for Micah but didn't see him.

"You're with us," a girl with auburn hair said to Cassie. "I'm Andi, remember?" Cassie recalled the blur of a girl who'd introduced herself quickly outside the C.I.T. bunk.

"Sure," Cassie said, relieved to be with someone she sort of knew.

"And there's one more," Andi said. "Where is he?" She shaded her eyes to search the crowded beach.

Cassie's stomach sunk. It would be just her

luck to have to work all night with the guy who'd witnessed her first mortifying moment of the summer. She felt sure he would be the one, so sure—until Andi started yelling out a name and Micah wasn't it.

"Charlie! Did you get lost or something?"

A floppy-haired guy came up. He was probably sixteen, the same age as Cassie, but there was something a little off about him, making him seem out of place on the island. It was like that song from way back on *Sesame Street*, about how one of these things is not like the other . . . He was that thing not like the other. All the other C.I.T.s—guys, girls—were tanned and fit and wearing swimsuits and shorts, and Charlie was exceptionally pale and skinny. Plus, he was wearing long pants. It was an understatement to say he stood out. He was cute, at least to someone who was into skinny pale boys in pants, which, surely people somewhere, in less sunny climates, were.

"I'm Charlie," he said, holding a hand out to Cassie. She didn't know exactly what to do with the hand—shaking it seemed so formal—but that's what he did, rigorously up and down, like they were thirty years old and at a business convention. "We're on fire duty," he added.

Cassie found out what that meant soon enough. She, Andi, and Charlie were the three C.I.T.s in charge of keeping the bonfires burning, which takes wood, lots of wood, and isn't as easy as it sounds, especially if the closest you've ever been to a fire was spicy chili or a sunburn.

Cassie kept lugging loads of firewood to the beach, her arms aching. As she worked, she saw the counselors and junior counselors—not that she knew their names, thanks to missing orientation—chatting each other up by the bonfires. She saw the campers downing their volcanic punch, throwing their Frisbees, playing their getting-to-know-you games. And she saw all the other C.I.T.s busting their butts making the whole thing happen.

At least that's what it felt like to Cassie. She kept passing Tori and her friends, who had formed a circle for some game involving peanut M&Ms that Tori had instigated. She told them that she first played it at her old bug-infested summer camp in Pennsylvania. Basically, each girl had grabbed a handful of candy and now she had to tell as many things about herself as she had M&Ms in her hands. Tori waved Cassie

41

over whenever she passed, but in a way Cassie was relieved she wasn't in that circle, her hand loaded down with M&Ms. She didn't feel so much like talking about herself. Maybe lugging around firewood wasn't such a bad gig after all.

Cassie was coming out of the woods when Andi joined her. "We have to be really careful back here," Andi said. She leaned in and whispered: "Two words: Wild. Boars."

Cassie just shook her head. "You're joking, right?"

"I know for a fact you have them on this island," Andi said, eyes widening. "My uncle traveled to Big Island in, like, 1984 and he slept on the beach and woke up surrounded by these huge monstrous pigs. They ate his breakfast, flattened his tent, and stole his socks. Dude, I am not kidding. In Minnesota, we've got deer. Here in Hawaii, you have to look out for, you know, pigs. But the rest of the island's nice, really." Andi elbowed Cassie hard. "Cassie, joke! It's gorgeous here. I love your island."

Andi grabbed some wood from Cassie's arms so she didn't have to hold it all.

"But you've been to Ohana before," Cassie said,

"last summer, right? And no attack of the wild boars then, right?"

"Yeah, yeah, that's what everyone says, but I play it safe, you know? Maybe you *don't* know. You don't seem like someone who would play it safe."

"What do you mean?" Cassie said.

There was a pause while they heaved the rest of the wood into the pile. Cassie bent over and caught her breath. When she came up for air, Andi was staring at her curiously in the flickering firelight. "I remember when you came with the other pro surfers last year. Did that big demonstration . . ."

In the near distance Cassie could hear the campers having a blast—everyone all relaxed and just excited to be a kid, she guessed. She never did any of that when she was younger. She sort of skipped all that stuff to compete. Maybe it would have been fun.

"I wish I could surf," Andi said. "I mean I can, *technically*, but not like you."

Cassie didn't comment.

"You're really good," Andi said.

"I guess I was," Cassie said so quietly she wondered if she'd said it out loud.

Andi nodded. "Definitely," she said. "Definitely. But what do you mean *was*?"

"Was what?"

"You said you were good—like, you're not anymore?"

Did that slip out? Cassie thought. She hadn't meant to talk in the past tense. Before she could try to explain herself, Charlie came running up with a bucket. He dumped the bucket on the fire, drowning out the flames and splashing a good backwash on his sneakers in the process.

"*What* did you just do?" Andi cried. "Charlie, the wood's all wet now. You can't build a fire with wet wood! Where do you come from, anyway?"

"New Mexico," he said, confused. What had been the bonfire was now a pool of black soot. Cassie noticed that the campers, counselors, and C.I.T.s all seemed to be packing up, as if the bonfire was over, but Andi had her back to the crowd and couldn't see.

"So didn't they teach you how to build fires in New Mexico or what?"

"Sure," Charlie said, "in Boy Scouts."

"He does this and he was a Boy Scout!" Andi shrieked, turning to Cassie. "Cassie, explain it to him."

Cassie glanced back at the crowds . . . the bonfire was undeniably breaking up for the night. "I think all Charlie was doing was—" Cassie started to explain.

But Andi broke in, impatient. "If you dump water on a fire, it goes out," she said.

Charlie spoke up. "Andi, the bonfire's over. Simona said we're on cleanup now. That means putting the fires *out*."

It took a second for it to sink in. Then Andi grinned. "Why didn't you say so?!"

Charlie shrugged. "Simona says we have to carry all the wood back."

"You have got to be kidding!" Andi said. She turned to Cassie. "Ah well. Tomorrow we'll be in the water, and that's all that matters." Then she winked at Charlie. "All except you, of course."

"I work in the office," Charlie explained to Cassie. "But maybe this summer I'll learn to surf or something." He went off, leaving Andi and Cassie alone again.

"So back to what we were talking about," Andi said. "What happened? You're not good at surfing anymore?"

Cassie shrugged. She wasn't sure what to say. Finally she just mumbled, "I don't know, I guess I'm the same as last year." Another shrug. Eyes darting. Hands knotted together. It would be a miracle if Andi didn't see that something was up.

Cassie got her miracle. Because Andi started talking, quickly as usual, and it seemed, for some long moments, that she really didn't think there was anything odd about what Cassie had said.

"Good," Andi was saying, "because I remember the expo last year. You were awesome out there. You caught this one wave and it curled over your head and you sort of crouched down and it looked like you were riding *inside* the wave, it was insane. I water-ski, and I'm also pretty good on a wakeboard, but put me on one of those big boards you were riding and I tip over, serious! Anyway, what's it like? Being pro, I mean. It must be, like, the best thing ever."

"It's cool," Cassie admitted. "It's like a dream. You travel a lot. And all you're supposed to do is surf. It's like someone's paying me to do *this*?"

Andi shook her head. "Wow," she breathed. "Tell me more." She seemed genuinely curious.

Maybe because of that Cassie felt able to talk to her—just as long as the topic didn't shift to what she was still hoping to avoid. So she told Andi what it was like, ever since she'd started surfing the junior circuit. She talked all about being on a surf team and having a sponsor like Coco Beach, the company that sent her free clothes and surfboards, just so she could be seen using and wearing their stuff, like a walking advertisement. She found herself talking about how weird it was not to be traveling and surfing with the rest of her team right now, like, what was she supposed to do with herself this summer? Like, what do *normal* people do, someone tell her please! She said that and then clammed up. It had come out all wrong. She'd probably sounded like a snob or a social reject. Or worse: a snobby social reject.

Andi leaned in. Before she opened her mouth, Cassie knew she'd ask the big question, the one everyone was curious about. And who could blame her?

"So, what are you doing here at camp, anyway?" Andi said. "I mean, shouldn't you be, like, training, or competing, or *something*?"

Cassie started to explain, "I—I'm just taking a break."

Cassie looked around the beach for Tori—her cousin was the only person here who knew why she was taking a break. But Tori must have gone back to her bunk; besides, Tori wouldn't tell Cassie's secret anytime soon.

"But why?" Andi said.

Cassie's head filled with any number of reasons: *I was tired of competing*—not true, not exactly. *I don't want to surf anymore*—a flat-out lie. Or just simply the catch-all reason that was no reason at all, *Why not?*

But she didn't have to settle on any of them. Charlie was back, this time with an armload of beach umbrellas. "Uh," he mumbled behind all the umbrellas, "help?"

Cassie jumped to his aid. So did Andi. By the time they put the umbrellas away and got all the chairs stacked, the campers had already been sent off for lights-out. It was time for the C.I.T.s to gather in the rec hall for their own set of activities.

"You'll love this," Andi said, grabbing Cassie's arm. "It's, like, an Ohana tradition. Now that we're C.I.T.s, we get to play."

"Play what?" Cassie said, getting caught up in the excitement.

"Truth or dare," Andi said, a twinkle in her blue-green eyes. "The C.I.T.s always play it the first night of camp."

"Oh, cool," Cassie said, though she did not feel in any way cool about it. Truth or dare was all about doing stupid things and revealing mushy and mega-embarrassing secrets. Not that Cassie would mind a dare, no matter how stupid. It was "truth" she was worried about.

Three

A game of truth or dare on the first night of the summer was definitely an Ohana C.I.T. ritual. When Danica had been an Ohana camper, she'd heard rumors of outrageous confessions and ridiculous dares worthy of some new Bam Margera MTV spin-off. Now, as a C.I.T. for the first time ever, Danica wanted to make sure her group of C.I.T.s lived up to the legends of those who came before. But her interest in this particular game of truth or dare went way beyond whatever so-called legends there were to live up to. Right now, her heart was beating just a little faster at the opportunity to go after "truth" with Micah. She had questions. Like, was he into her again? Did he want to start something up like last summer? Could he forgive her for dumping him? And, worse, for doing it in that note? For not calling or e-mailing to apologize? For no Facebook or a MySpace comments all year like he didn't even exist? Could he?

Yeah, so many questions. With "truth," she might be able to get an answer or two.

She'd dressed carefully for the night. Of course, the outfit she'd worn to work at the luau was the one she still had on for the game, and between then and now she'd somehow come away with a few lava-colored stains on her white bikini top and white skirt. This was thanks to manning the volcanic punch station all evening—she should have known that stuff would stain. She should never have worn white!

She was considering running back to the bunk to change, but she didn't want to lose her spot at the choice picnic table or, worse, come back all sweaty from the run. Then she considered sending one of her friends—Sasha or Sierra, both C.I.T.s with her this year—back to the bunk to grab her a shirt. The C.I.T. bunk was maybe a ten-minute sprint there and back from the rec hall, where the truth-or-dare game was to take place. She'd have a shirt in no time . . .

Then she saw him—Micah. He said "Hey," and she said "Hey," and he was wearing a black T-shirt and his hair was longer this year and she couldn't take her eyes off him and she forgot about the mess of her outfit for the moment.

She hadn't told Sasha or Sierra that she wanted Micah back. She could just imagine the conversation:

"But *you* dumped *him*."

"Yeah, I know that but—"

"And you said he was *boring*."

"Yeah, I did say that but—"

"You said you could do *better*."

She knew exactly what Sasha and Sierra would say: They'd repeat back to her everything she'd said at the end of last summer, and probably worse things she didn't even remember saying. They wouldn't understand that maybe—just maybe—she'd changed her mind about Micah. Like maybe she spent all year thinking about him. Feeling stupid. Regretting what she'd done.

Not that she was 100 percent sure—or even 75 percent sure—she wanted to be his girlfriend again. But it wasn't something she *didn't* want. *Let's just say I'm open*, she thought. *And it all depends on whether Micah's open to it, too.* Confiding in Sierra and Sasha about it, even though they were her closest friends at camp, would just complicate the issue. Besides, if Micah wasn't interested, no one could know she was first.

The C.I.T.s were all gathered in the rec hall, a sheltered structure used for activities and meals when it rained. There was a thatched roof but no walls. The giant room was open to the beach and, in the darkness, the hush and roar of the ocean. This was one of many places on the Ohana campus that Danica loved. But she wasn't at all sentimental about it—she just made sure to snag the picnic table with the best view and perch herself on top. Sasha and Sierra scrambled up beside her. It was easy for Danica to slip back into her old role: the camp VIP, the one everyone wanted to hang with. Who cared if she had only a few friends back home in Florida? Here, everyone loved her.

Danica gazed around at the group of kids she'd be spending this summer with. She avoided looking again at Micah. Besides him, there were the usual sports fiends, the summer beach bums, and the spoiled rich kids getting a paid vacay to learn how to surf so they didn't stay at home and take up shoplifting. Some familiar faces, too.

Sierra and Sasha, of course. Sierra was from Cali, and Sasha from Texas—they came to Ohana every year, and they always had Danica's back.

Then there was Emmy, a local Hawaiian, and not even a C.I.T.—she was just a lifeguard. Still, she was nice, and knew Danica well enough not to ever cross her. Danica gave Emmy a wave but didn't scoot over to give her a spot on her picnic table. Charlie was the guy working in the office this summer, poor stiff. Then there was Ben, the new guy—blond, buff, tanned—that all the girls seemed to have their eye on. He was so full of himself, Danica just couldn't see the attraction. Some other C.I.T.s were there; Danica looked them all over—*shrug*. No one here could compete with her for Micah.

Notably missing from the group was Andi—she was from some landlocked state that Danica always forgot the name of. But the thing about Andi was that she was excessively good at whatever she did. The girl could Jet Ski and water-ski like she had a lake in her backyard. Which very well might be the case. Rumor was her parents were rich enough—so maybe she did. Also, even though she talked entirely too much, she was really pretty, with her curly red hair and her long legs and . . . let's just say Danica hoped she wasn't Micah's type.

Still, there was one other notable person missing from the rec hall. "Where's that surfer girl?" Sasha asked Danica. "I thought you said she was a C.I.T."

"Is she a surfing C.I.T.?" Sierra asked innocently enough, but just the question itself put Danica on edge. She'd been trying to block out what the surfer girl had said when she was signing in: *I changed my mind.*

She'd said that about being the surfing C.I.T. Like she'd been a shoo-in for the surf spot but was all, *Oh, let some other girl take it, I'm sooo bored.*

Did she think being the surfing C.I.T. was beneath her? Was that it?

"She has to be a surfing C.I.T.," Sasha was saying. "That would be, like, so wrong if she wasn't. Maybe we have three surfing C.I.T.s this summer. That would make sense, right, Danica?"

"No, it would not make sense," Danica said. She was trying to keep all expression from her face.

Sierra and Sasha met eyes—they knew her pretty well; maybe they could see right through her.

"What did you say her name was again, Danica?" Sierra said.

Danica really did not want to say the name. It was bad enough she had to compete with the girl, an actual pro surfer, when *she* had always been the best surfer at camp. (Not to mention body-boarder, swimmer, Jet Skier—you name it, Danica killed at it.) But now they had to go on talking about the girl like she was some celebrity. Well, she was not.

Sasha and Sierra were waiting for her answer. "Her name is Cassie," Danica said at last. "Cassie Hamilton." She'd seen the pictures in the surf magazines. She'd read the articles about how the girl had won her first contest at age twelve. Cassie Hamilton, Cassie Hamilton, Cassie Hamilton. Not a bona fide celebrity, but still . . . *Just my luck she's here this summer*, Danica thought.

"Cassie, that's right!" Sasha said. "Where is she, anyway?"

"How would I know?" Danica snapped.

Sasha shrugged.

Danica gazed out at the small crowd in the rec hall, effectively ending the conversation. C.I.T.s were sprawled out on the benches, some lying on top of the picnic tables, some stretched out on the floor. The room was lit only by lanterns that bobbed in the wind, giving the scene a disembodied glow. "Let's start!" she called out suddenly, silencing the chatter. "Latecomers'll just get the worst dares."

"The really disgusting ones!" Sasha chirped.

"Yeah, let's start the game!" Emmy yelled.

That's when Andi walked in the rec hall, Cassie in tow. Andi got waylaid by the door, and Danica noticed that Cassie was left to find a seat on her own. Danica made sure to watch her the whole way down the length of the floor, looking wildly around for someone she recognized—probably no one—seeking out an empty seat at one of the picnic tables—none were left—till she just chose a spot near the edge of the circle, on the floor. Danica elbowed Sierra and Sasha. "Look who's here," she whispered.

"I like her shirt," Sierra said. It was sleeveless, pale blue, nothing special.

Danica gave her a look as if to say, *No you don't*. But as she did, she noticed someone else admiring Cassie's shirt—or worse—the person inside the shirt. Micah. He was at a picnic table across from Cassie, looking right at her.

Then—horrors—Cassie was looking back.

Danica got a sinking feeling. Did they, like, *like* each other or something?

This would mess with all of Danica's plans. This would send her world spinning. Sure, she thought there was a chance that Micah might not be into her again, not at first. She knew it could take some time, some effort. But she didn't expect someone else to get in the way, not so soon.

"C'mon, let's start the game," Ben said. "Truth or dare, who's first?"

"Hey, Cassie," Danica said before she thought it through. "You go first."

Cassie flinched, turned pale. All eyes in the rec hall were on her. "Me?" she said. "I don't think I've ever played this game before . . ."

"Sure you have," Ben said. "Who hasn't?"

Cassie shrugged, eyes at the floor. Danica watched her carefully, trying to see through the innocent act to what was really going on in there.

"Don't worry," Andi told Cassie, taking a seat on the edge of Danica's picnic table. "You'll love this game. It's fun."

Danica gave a well contained smile. "Truth or dare, Cassie?" she said lightly.

Danica wanted her to say truth, and she wanted to ask the question. The girl was hiding something—she could see it plain as a bright, hot Hawaii day.

But Cassie didn't give her a chance. "Dare," she said too quickly. She looked up, gazing around at the circle of C.I.T.s, her eyes settling at last on Danica. "Dare," she repeated, this time with determination.

Something inside Danica clicked. It was her comfort zone, being in control like this. Putting someone in their place, letting them know who was the real someone to watch around here. Call it a defense mechanism, call it whatever. But sometimes, when Danica was feeling threatened and off-kilter and uncomfortable in her clothes and unsure of where she stood, sometimes she acted the only way she could act. That is, mean. Who wouldn't do the same if they could?

She gazed back at Cassie and contemplated her many options. *Dare, it is.*

Cassie chose dare. She had to. It was bad enough Danica had picked her to go first, but for Cassie to get truth and end up somehow revealing her secret straightaway, in front of all these kids she barely knew . . . who wouldn't pick dare over truth in her shoes?

When she said she wanted a dare, all the other C.I.T.s in the rec hall let out a great, long "Ooooooooooooooooh." Clearly, they were trying to make her nervous.

"Hold it!" Danica called out from across the circle. "It's Cassie's first night here—her dare's got to be something *good*." Her eyes narrowed, and it occurred to Cassie that this particular dare might mean way more to Danica than any harmless "fun."

Is it what I said about the surfing C.I.T. position? Cassie wondered. She should be more careful when she talked about surfing here—she didn't want anyone to think she was bragging. Especially after what happened a few months ago . . . now who would walk around bragging about that?

She glanced away from Danica and—*zing!*—met eyes with Micah, who was sitting on a picnic bench nearby. This kept happening. She'd look somewhere and end up in an eye lock with him. Now his lips twitched in a small smile and instead of smiling back she pulled her gaze away. She forced herself to turn back to Danica, to be sentenced with whatever dare they'd choose for her, and go on and get it over with.

Danica was across the rec hall, sitting atop a picnic table with Andi and two other friends. Their C.I.T. leis said Sierra and Sasha. Sierra had long, dark hair and Sasha had a cute chestnut brown bob. They were exceptionally pretty, of course, just like Danica. The four girls huddled together, whispering. Cassie, sitting on the floor on the other side of the room, felt very alone. Andi had been friendly enough at the bonfire, but clearly she was way better friends with Danica. Cassie found herself wishing that her cousin were here for the game. *If only Tori was a C.I.T.*, she thought. *Why does she have to be just fourteen!*

"C'mon!" one of the other C.I.T.s called out. "Pick a dare already!"

Suddenly, Sasha leaped up from the huddle. "I have Cassie's dare!" she cried. "I just thought of it. Okay, Cassie, you go to the camp kitchen. You break in however you can, 'cause they lock it up at night. And you bring us something for dessert. Go!"

That's it? Cassie thought. What with all the hype, she figured they'd go for something at least a hair more . . . dangerous. She'd never done any breaking-and-entering before, but this dare at least seemed harmless.

In fact, Danica seemed disappointed. "Sasha!" she hissed. "I said not that one!"

"I'm hungry," Sasha said with a shrug.

"Fine," Danica said. Her bright, intensely fake smile turned in a flash on Cassie. "You heard the dare," she said. "So go."

Cassie stood. All eyes were on her, but this was nothing, nothing at all.

All she said was, "Where's the kitchen?" She was pointed in its direction and went off to find it. It turned out that the door, though locked, had an open window just beside it, so it was easy to get in and out without any broken glass or forced dead bolts. When she returned to the rec hall it was with an armful of whipped cream cans that were passed around the circle and sprayed into everyone's mouth. The "dessert" was a big hit with the C.I.T.s, all except for Danica. Cassie noticed that when a whipped cream can came her way, she wrinkled her nose and waved it on to the next person like she was being asked to eat a mouthful of insecticide.

Now that Cassie had gotten her dare over with, she began to relax. That's when the game got interesting. It all started when the lifeguard, Emmy, was dared to spend five minutes alone with one of the guys and "whatever happens" behind closed doors "happens."

"With who?" Emmy said. She crossed her arms over her chest, clearly not pleased by the dare. But seeing as this was the first night of camp, it was not a good idea to back out of a dare in front of the other C.I.T.s, even Cassie could see that.

"Me," said a voice. Ben stepped up and did a half bow like he was being all gallant. From the way she'd heard other girls talk about him, Cassie knew he was considered one of the cutest guys at camp. Problem is, he sure acted like he knew it. In Cassie's eyes, this made him, like, twelve times *less* attractive.

Emmy made a face as Ben took her hand, but Cassie thought it was all for show. Something told her—the flush creeping up Emmy's cheeks maybe?— that Emmy was psyched beyond belief to spend some time alone in a dark room with Ben. Even if the room itself was the supply closet crammed full of brooms, mops, buckets, and broken surfboards. Cassie watched with curiosity as Emmy and Ben entered the dark closet and closed the door behind them. Then all was quiet.

Is this what normal kids did? Forced each other into confined spaces with the lights off while everyone stood outside trying to listen in? It seemed absurd.

Cassie realized she'd missed out on a lot of things by becoming a pro surfer so young—there just hadn't been time for games like this. Then again, maybe it was a good thing that she'd avoided being imprisoned in a closet. So far, at least.

After Emmy and Ben emerged from the closet— amid giggles and fruitless shouted requests to reveal what went on in there—the game took a turn for truth. Danica's truth revealed she was single. So did Andi's, though she said that what she had back at home was "complicated." Truth revealed that Charlie had never been in a relationship, like, ever. (*Me either*, Cassie thought but didn't say out loud.) Sasha and Sierra were both fresh from breakups. They wanted to keep things open for the summer, they said. Ben didn't have a girlfriend—neither did Micah. Pretty much everyone was single and wanted the whole room of C.I.T.s to know it. Cassie figured that would be her question, too. Did she have a boyfriend? That's an easy one! No.

Then again, they could ask her something else. She had a sinking feeling they would. So when it was Cassie's turn once more, she opened her mouth and found herself saying, "Dare." Again.

"What, are you afraid of truth or something?" Danica called. Probably she'd meant it as a joke— like, Ha-ha! She doesn't want anyone to know she's single!—but Cassie couldn't keep her face neutral. Something twitched. Something gave her away. And she knew Danica saw it.

"No, I just want another dare," Cassie said quietly.

"Five minutes in the closet with . . ." Danica started, making a big show of looking around the circle at all the C.I.T.s on offer. Her eyes lingered on Micah. Cassie could see that's where her eyes were lingering, and, knowing this, having the possibility dangled out before her, Cassie found herself feeling something she could only call strange. Something was making itself known in her chest. A physical something. It was weird and fluttery, like a living creature hopping around inside her chest.

Excitement—that's what it felt like, the way surfing used to be. She'd never felt anything close to that in relation to a boy. Why in the world did she feel *excited* to be locked in a supply closet with Micah?

But before Cassie could wrap her brain around this revelation, Danica pulled her eyes away from Micah and settled them on someone else. This new guy of choice was the plainest, skinniest, most pasty guy in the room. "Five minutes in the closet with *Charlie!*" Danica announced. Then she winked at Cassie as if to say, *Have fun!*

Inexplicably, Cassie felt disappointed. She tried to keep that off her face. Charlie had stood up. He was holding a hand out to her. What else could she do but take it?

Once the closet door was closed, the lights down, they each found a place on the grimy floor. Cassie couldn't see, but it felt like something sloshing and wet was just beside her. A bucket of mop water? It did smell a lot like Lysol.

"So, I guess we're supposed to, um . . ." Charlie said.

She couldn't see him in the dark, but she moved her foot and it seemed to hit his foot. "I guess, I mean I've never done this before—" Cassie meant not just sitting in a dark Lysol-scented closet with a strange boy, but the *this* that made it so she had to stop talking. She was sixteen and she'd never actually kissed a boy before. Strike that. Because now, in the dark of this closet, it was suddenly actually happening.

In the deep darkness, Charlie had somehow found her face. His mouth touched hers and held onto it for some long seconds. She kissed back for some more seconds, but it felt forced, it felt too weird for words—it also somehow tasted of Lysol. Cassie pulled away at the same moment he did. Awkward.

Then they both sat there in the dark, trying to silently wipe the other's spit from their chins, except that when she lifted her arm to wipe her mouth he also lifted his arm to do the same. They ended up hitting each other and then apologizing profusely. All that took up a whole minute. Then he said:

"You know, we don't have to do this."

"We can just say we did," Cassie said. "If they ask . . ."

"Yeah."

"Yeah."

Good, we're in agreement on that, at least, Cassie thought with relief.

"I should tell you I'm sort of taken," Charlie said then.

"You have a girlfriend? I thought, out there, I thought you said you didn't."

"I don't," he said. "Not exactly. But there's someone here I . . . you know."

There was a moment of quiet between them. Outside the closet they could hear the other C.I.T.s talking, laughing. Maybe they forgot Cassie and Charlie were in here.

"Who?" she said. *Danica,* she thought immediately. She was so pretty—probably all the guys were crushing on Danica.

But Charlie said, "Andi."

"Oh," she breathed.

"But please don't tell her, okay?"

"I won't. I swear."

"Good, because I have no idea what she'd think,

you know? She was looking at me before across the circle, but maybe she was just, I don't know, *looking* at me?" He seemed a bit lovesick. Cassie thought it was adorable.

She spent so much of her time surfing—her whole life, it seemed—that she never had time to like someone that much. *What would that feel like?* she was wondering when, without warning, a face came to her mind. Micah's face.

But along with that face came the memory of a certain gold bathing suit and just as quickly both thoughts were banished from her mind. She and Charlie spent the rest of their time in the supply closet talking about Andi—about how nice she seemed, how cheerful she was, how she was a good wakeboarder. Cassie imagined that Charlie could talk about Andi for hours if she let him.

When they emerged from the closet, the game of truth or dare was in full swing. Apparently, Ben had chosen dare, and Danica had just finished telling him what the dare would be.

"What do you think, Benny, brave enough to take that one on?" Danica said.

Cassie and Charlie took their places back in

the circle—no one had even asked what happened in the closet. Either they assumed it was nothing worth mentioning or they were just too preoccupied with Ben's dare.

Cassie, for her part, wondered what the dare was. Her eyes shot to Ben. He was standing up, in the middle of the circle of C.I.T.s, his overly bright smile faltering, just a little. "I'll do it," he said. With that, he ran off.

"Where's he going?" Cassie asked a C.I.T. who sat near her.

"The kitchen," the C.I.T. said, eyes twinkling.

As they waited for Ben's return, Sierra turned to Danica. "You're not serious about this, are you?" she asked.

Danica just shrugged. "That's up to Ben."

"Raw meat is gross," said Sasha with a shudder.

"Actually, it's not just gross, it's sort of dangerous," Emmy said.

A shiver ran down Cassie's spine. *Wait—what are they talking about?* She scanned the crowd, trying to make sense of it. "What's going on?" she whispered.

70

But the C.I.T. beside her shushed her. Ben had just come back, raw meat bulging disgustingly from his shorts pockets.

"Ben, maybe you shouldn't—" Emmy started to say.

"What do you know about it?" Danica was saying to Emmy. "Go swimming with hamburgers much?"

Swimming? Hamburgers? Cassie thought in alarm. She froze.

Emmy fumbled on her words but continued. "It's just that, I mean, sharks are rare on Big Island, but they are out there. It's not unheard of. My brother knows some guy whose cousin got bit, seriously. And sharks are attracted to raw meat—animal and human and hamburger. They have, like, a meat radar from, like, hundreds of miles away, I think, I mean I swear I heard that—"

Ben clapped his hands, cutting her off. "Well, I love me some hamburger. Let's do it." And before there was time to argue he'd run off toward the crashing waves in the near distance.

That's when Cassie found her feet. Suddenly she was up and running. She knew she was overreacting, but she couldn't stop herself. It was like she'd been separated from her body. Like someone had taken control of her legs and was using them to sprint out of the rec hall and across the sand toward this guy she didn't even know, all because she heard something about sharks and meat and had to stop it.

But maybe she wasn't overreacting. Cassie thought the whole idea of putting raw meat in someone's pockets and telling them to jump in the ocean at night was just so *not funny*. She didn't care who it was—egotistical Ben with the flashy smiles full of teeth or Charlie or whoever. Maybe Danica thought the hamburger thing was just some dumb prank, but it could actually be deadly if he went through with it. Sharks *are*, in fact, attracted to raw meat—anyone could look up that piece of information on Wikipedia. *Is everyone insane?* Cassie wondered.

"Ben!" she called. "Hold up!" She reached him on the beach at the point where the tides were crawling up onto the sand. She grabbed his arm. Would she dive in after him if he was fool enough to go in? Dude, she hoped not.

"Hey there," Ben said. "Cassie, right? You coming in with me?" He probably figured she had a crush on him, that that's why she'd run after him. *Great.*

Standing so close to Ben like this, she realized how it might look to anyone else. All the other C.I.T.s probably figured she had a crush on him, too.

Also, standing so close to Ben, she noticed one other thing: He smelled. Not like cologne straight out of *GQ*, but like meat. She stepped back. It was times like these that she considered becoming a vegetarian.

"No," Cassie said, trying to explain. "Just don't do it. I don't want you to."

"You're saying you don't want me to go in the water," Ben said.

"That's what I'm saying."

"You're saying you're worried about me."

"I guess," Cassie said reluctantly. "I guess that's what I'm saying."

"I kind of like that," he said. "For you, I won't go in. Feel better?"

"Yeah, thanks," she said. She was feeling very, very silly now for running after him.

"Good," he said. "I'm glad you feel better." Then he was—oh no—putting his arm around her.

73

Beautiful. Now I'll smell like beef, she thought.

This was getting blown up all wrong—she'd just wanted to stop the stupid dare, not make Ben think she liked him. She shrugged off his arm and headed back for the rec hall. The rest of the C.I.T.s were standing on the edge of the room, watching.

"What was that about?" Danica said, narrowing her eyes at Cassie.

Ben answered for her. "I'm not going through with it," he said. "Cassie thinks it's too dangerous. So what should I do instead? Eat the meat and risk salmonella?"

Danica wrinkled her nose. "Just get rid of it," she said. "You smell. Besides, you get salmonella poisoning from *chicken*." She rolled her eyes.

Ben dumped out the contents of his pockets in the trash. Cassie noticed that he kept looking right at her. He really thought she liked him. The idea was so ridiculous she wanted to laugh. She met Micah's eyes and then pulled away quickly.

It was her turn next.

"Dare," she said. "Just as long as it has nothing to do with hamburgers."

"You can't have three dares in a row," Danica said. "Game rules."

"Really?" Sasha said. "I didn't know that was in the rules . . ." She trailed off at the look Danica gave her.

"Fine," Danica said. "She can have a dare if she wants a dare. How about this—it's a good one—your dare is *truth*."

"Truth, truth, truth, truth, truth," the chant echoed around the circle. Cassie took a seat on the floor. She felt heavy, stuck in place. Being in the closet with Charlie hadn't been this uncomfortable.

"Let me ask the question," Danica said. She brushed her stick-straight blond hair over one shoulder and shot a long look at Cassie. "Sierra, could you bring me my bag?"

Sierra obediently handed it over.

Danica fished around in the bag until she came up with a magazine. It looked like *Teen Vogue*, but Cassie didn't catch the cover. Danica shook some sand out of it and then flipped through until she found a page. She held it out, spread flat, showing the Coco Beach ad.

Cassie knew just the one it would be. It was

some surfer girls from her team standing around on the sand, boards poking skyward, hair still wet from the sea. Cassie was in the middle, the only one of the girls not smiling. She had this dead serious look on her face. All the girls had quotes under their pictures. Cassie's read: *Competition is my life.* And the word *life* was underlined, six times, to show she really meant it. And she had meant it, she had, at the moment when that photo was taken. It was just a few months ago, but it felt like a lifetime.

"Obviously this is you," Danica said, waving the page around. "So tell us the truth, Cassie, if competition is your *life*, then what are you doing here?"

"I'm a C.I.T.," Cassie said, just stating the obvious. But she knew even as she said it that Danica wouldn't let up.

And she didn't. "We know you surf the big-time," Danica continued. "And we know that big-time surfers don't just chuck it all to go to summer camp. So what is this, some kind of joke to you?"

"It's not a joke," Cassie said. Her voice came out softer than she meant it to.

She wasn't about to make a big deal of it. So she

surfed. So she surfed at big contests for money. So she'd won a few times. So she had a big-deal sponsor like Coco Beach. So what. It's not like she wanted to go around Ohana bragging about it.

"Nice bikini," Ben said, taking a closer look at the ad.

Cassie rolled her eyes.

Andi spoke up. "Wow, Cassie, it's like in *Blue Crush*. Not that you're a maid and clean hotel toilets"—she shuddered—"I just mean you must be really good."

"I've been surfing since I was seven," Cassie said with a shrug. "I went pro when I was twelve. I've always surfed. So, yeah I'm good." She didn't mean that to come across as arrogant, but she realized that maybe it did. "I mean I hope so," she added. "I hope I'm good."

"Oh, you're good. No argument there," Andi continued. "But Danica does sort of have a point. Like I was asking you before, what *are* you doing here, anyway?"

"It's wack when you think about it," Ben cut in. "Pro surfers travel all over the world. There's a competition every week. Who takes a break to go to camp? Not that this place isn't awesome, so don't throw anything at me, Danica, but still."

"*Wack* isn't a word I'd use, but it is strange," Charlie chimed in. He met Cassie's eyes and shrugged.

"Yeah," said Sasha.

"Yeah," said Sierra.

All eyes were on Cassie. What did they want her to say? *Yes, I'm a total freak? I gave up a surfing career so I could go camp, hey could you pass me that marshmallow?*

Micah spoke for the first time. "Did something happen?" he asked her.

Cassie had planned to avoid answering that question all together, but the fact that Micah was the one to ask made her unable to ignore it. "The truth is, well, what's going on is that I'm here because I'm taking a break because"—here Cassie paused—"because I had an accident." She looked out across the circle and there was Micah. She shrugged. She wanted it to seem like no big deal, but it was obviously a big deal. She wouldn't be here taking a break otherwise.

"You wet your pants in the water," Ben shot out. "I knew I wasn't the only one who pees in the ocean."

"Ewwwww," Andi said. "Guess who I'm not swimming next to ever again."

"Not that kind of accident," Cassie said. "Look, why are we talking about this? It was nothing, seriously. Truth or dare, who's next?"

Danica raised her hand, though clearly not to volunteer. "But now you got me all curious about the accident," she said. "Did you, like, lose an arm or something?"

"A boat!" Sierra shouted. "Did you fall off a boat?"

"I bet it was a Jet Ski. *Everyone* falls off Jet Skis," Sasha said.

"No, no, something way bigger . . . I know, an airplane! A plane, like, fell out of the sky and landed on you, but you escaped."

"That doesn't make any sense, Sierra. She would have been crushed or blown up into little bits and then she wouldn't have *any* legs."

"True. So she forgot how to swim, because she got amnesia, and she drowned!"

"Obviously she didn't drown because she's sitting right here."

"*Almost* drowned."

The reasons were getting ridiculous. Cassie was waiting to hear alien abduction next. But then Emmy was the one to say it: "Shark attack," she said. "It was, wasn't it? That's why you were so totally freaked out about Ben going in the water."

"I knew it," Ben said.

"You did not," Danica said.

"I would've figured it out," he insisted.

"So was it a shark, really?" Emmy said to Cassie.

And Cassie just couldn't keep it off her face. This was the truth part of the game, after all. And even if her mouth opened up to deny it, her expression would have shown the truth of what happened.

How she'd been on her board, out in the water. It was way early in the morning, and she was doing what she usually did before she even ate breakfast— seeking a good wave. She'd already gotten one wave that morning—a big one, and it slammed her. She'd rolled and spluttered and hit something hard with her foot, but she was fearless, after all. She wouldn't let anything stop her. So she got rolled, so what. She came back up for air, and she got back on her board, and she waited for the next wave.

And because of this, she should probably blame herself for what happened next. If she'd looked at her foot, if she'd let herself feel the pain, she would have seen that she'd scraped it up pretty badly on a rough patch of coral when she went down. She would have seen that she was bleeding. If she had been paying attention, she would have paddled in. Because that's what you do when you're bleeding—if there's any chance there could be a shark in the water, any chance at all, you head back, you paddle in.

But she hadn't been thinking. She hadn't cared about the pain in her foot; she'd hardly felt it. What she'd been so totally focused on was that she didn't want one bad wipeout to ruin her whole day. So she'd floated on her board, keeping an eye out for the next wave. And all the while her bad foot was dangling down in the water. Calling to whatever was down below.

Then it came. She didn't know how she saw it—this moving shadow, sinister, like an enemy submarine from a war movie. She had no clue what it was. But there was something in her, some reflex that knew to move her leg. She pulled her leg up onto her board just in time. When the shark came to the surface for a bite, it got the tail of her board instead. If she hadn't moved . . . If . . .

Here in the rec hall, with all the C.I.T.s staring at her, Cassie shook the memory away, trying not to think of it.

"*No. Way,*" Emmy said. "Where did it get you?" Her eyes were running up and down Cassie's body, trying to find some scar that no one had noticed before. Except there was no scar.

"Wait," Micah said. "Are you serious?" He had an incredulous look on his face. Like she should be dead, but by some weird miracle of the ocean, some senseless twist of fate, she was alive. Almost swallowed by a shark and yet somehow still here.

But that's the thing. She wasn't almost swallowed by a shark. It didn't actually bite her—it had taken a bite out of her board instead. And for some reason she couldn't bring herself to admit it, that nothing, in fact, had happened. So why was she so freaked out if nothing happened? It made no sense.

At this moment, Tori burst into the rec hall. She froze when she saw how quiet everyone was. "I thought you guys were playing a game," she said lamely. Then, "Please, please don't tell my counselor I snuck out, okay?"

With all eyes now on her, Tori tiptoed over to Cassie sat beside her on the floor. "I figured you'd need me," she whispered to Cassie. "Sure looks like it, too. They're serious about truth or dare here, huh?"

"Yeah," Cassie said. She motioned to the room. "I told them."

"You *told* them told them?" Tori said softly. "I thought you didn't want to tell anyone, Cass."

Cassie shrugged. "Well, I did," she said.

"Okay," Tori said tentatively. She put her arm around Cassie for support.

Cassie felt so stupid for taking this whole thing so seriously. Anyone else would have been: *Whoa, shark almost got my foot . . . didn't . . . cool, so where's the next wave?* But Cassie was traumatized. She remembered her board splitting in two and lots of screaming. Then this mad scramble in the water, the kids with her trying to get her on the board and back to shore, someone saying *Did it get her leg?, Did it get her leg?*, just saying that over and over so Cassie thought maybe it had, and then being on the sand, and all the faces hovering over her, and not being able to look, not wanting to see. And when she did, she saw that she still had her legs. Both of them. And her arms and everything else. She was fine, perfectly fine. There wasn't a scratch on her.

The other surfers there had laughed it off—though no one went back in the water. Once a shark is spotted, surfing is pretty much out for the rest of the day. Everyone said it was a bummer about her broken board, and that was that. No one—not her surfing friends, her teammates, her family, her coach—thought she'd be reluctant to get back on a board after that.

Because nothing happened! Cassie's mind shrieked at her.

She didn't want to tell this to the other C.I.T.s—it was bad enough they knew about the shark at all. But Tori didn't know what they'd heard so far. She must have thought they knew the whole story. So Tori said, "Yeah, it's lucky nothing happened."

Danica jumped on this right away. "What do you mean nothing happened? I thought there was a shark."

"There was a shark," Tori said, clearly confused.

"And the shark bit her . . ."

"No, it bit her board."

"So it didn't bite her?"

"No." Tori turned to Cassie, all confused. "What, didn't you tell them that?"

"Actually, she didn't," Danica said. "She made it sound like the shark chewed off her leg."

"It could have," Tori said, getting defensive. Cassie found herself unable to say much of anything, and she was grateful that her cousin was there. "She cut her foot," Tori said. "Sharks are drawn to the smell of blood, you know, it's like *science*. Cass escaped just in time. She could have been totally swallowed."

"But she wasn't," Danica said. "Nothing actually happened. Right, Cassie?"

Cassie opened her mouth. "Right," she found herself agreeing.

"I don't get it," Emmy cut in. "If nothing happened, then why stop surfing?"

"You don't think that would have been freaky?" Andi said. "I do. I would have been beyond freaked out for like *a week*."

Cassie cringed at that. For her, it had been four months.

85

Yeah, everyone was agreeing. Close call. Freaky. They seemed to understand. Hopefully they'd drop it and move on with the rest of the stupid game.

Danica didn't seem to want to let that happen. "I bet you're scared to go in the water at all," she said suddenly. "I would be. I'd be *petrified*."

"I go in the water," Cassie insisted.

"Yeah," Tori jumped in. "She's always in the water."

"Oh good," Danica said. "'Cause that would be a weird. A C.I.T. for swimming who's afraid, you know, of water."

Cassie stood. She wiped some whipped cream off her shirt. She looked out in the direction of the ocean, her home ocean . . . it was just like looking out on her own familiar street. Except, this street was filled with invisible breaks where you could get the leash to your surfboard caught and flail around and really almost drown—no joke, that happened to another surfer she knew—and with riptides that could pull you out faster than you wanted to go, and heavy waves that could throw your board out like a cannon, and killer animals that could creep up beneath you and swallow you whole . . .

"Nothing to worry about," Cassie said. She heard a big wave crashing out where she couldn't see it. "I'm not afraid of the water. I go in the water all the time."

Four

Cassie was used to getting up before the sun. That was the life of a surfer: stumbling out of bed while it was still dark, listening to the surf report to know where to get the best waves, grabbing a bathing suit, a board, heading for the water just as the first shock of light was peeking over the horizon. The waves weren't so packed then. There was quiet, this sense of peace. For Cassie, it was the only time surfing wasn't about trying to win.

Even after Cassie stopped surfing, she still found herself getting up around the same time. She didn't even need an alarm clock; her body was just used to it.

After her first night sleeping in the C.I.T. bunk with the other girls, Cassie opened her eyes at the crack of early as usual. Within minutes, she'd slipped out of the bunk and was on the sand, hand over her eyes, bathing suit on, looking out at the water. The sun was a brilliant orange, just beginning to rise. The swells were a good height. It was a perfect day for surfing. Not that Cassie was going to take advantage of it this morning.

She'd brought a board to Ohana, of course—how suspect would it have looked if she hadn't? But so far her new yellow board had stood there, poking out of the sand, untouched. Cassie left it where it was and started for the water. She'd swim, she figured. *That's what I'm here to do this summer . . . swim,* she thought. *No problem, right?*

But before she got even two feet in the wet sand, a voice was calling after her.

"Cassie, you forgot this!" She saw Andi running up, carrying both her own wakeboard and Cassie's yellow surfboard up over her head. Andi reached Cassie's spot in the sand and bent over, breathless. "Hey," she said. "Good idea to get up before everyone else. You don't mind if I join you, do you?"

"No, totally not," Cassie said.

"You weren't going to surf on the *camp* boards, were you?" Andi said, wrinkling her nose. "They're so gross."

"Nah," Cassie said. "I just forgot my board, I guess." She took it in her arms—it was so much heavier than she remembered.

Andi waded in the water, and Cassie followed, up to her waist. "So," Andi said.

"So . . ." Cassie responded. She did not want to have this conversation. Last night she'd said enough about what happened to last the whole summer. And, besides, sharks were one topic of conversation that was best avoided while out in the water.

But Andi had something else on her mind. "So spill: How was it with Charlie? Is he a good kisser or so-so or what?" Seeing the look on Cassie's face, Andi added, "C'mon, you were in that supply closet with him for, like, ever! I want details."

Cassie laughed. She couldn't help but think of Charlie's confession in the closet—how she knew he would have much rather been in there with Andi. "There's nothing much to tell, really," Cassie said. *Though there is, there is!* she thought. *But I promised Charlie I wouldn't.*

"That bad, huh?" Andi said.

"No!" Cassie didn't want to say anything bad about Charlie. He was actually pretty sweet and cool.

"No, I mean, I didn't get the chance to find out. He has his eye on someone else. Lucky girl."

And that girl happened to be standing next to her in the water. All Cassie had to do was ask, and she could find out for Charlie what Andi thought of him . . .

But Andi's attention was suddenly elsewhere.

"Ohmygodohmylookatthatwave, I'm going for it!" she shrieked, paddling ferociously. She caught the wave on her wakeboard and rode it into the distance. Cassie, for her part, sat straddling her surfboard, watching.

At least she was out on the water, even if she was just sitting there. In just a few hours she'd be assisting the swimming counselors with the campers. Hopefully all swimming instruction would take place in the pool at first. And no surfboards would be involved. But with Andi here, she didn't want to show what she'd been hiding last night. She'd ride a few waves, no biggie. Then she'd go on in, shower, get changed, and start her first day at Ohana.

Besides, Camp Ohana was on a part of the Kona beach not known for surfing. The waves here were small, for beginners. She was up for small now, so in a way it was perfect.

Even so, she let a good wave pass her by. Then another. She just sat astride her surfboard, watching them go.

Then she saw a really good one. She saw Andi catch it for a short time, then go under. Now it was headed Cassie's way, there for the taking. She began to run on instinct. Without thinking she was paddling for it, gaining speed, just at the point when she should jump up and ride it to wherever it took her . . .

But she didn't jump up. She hesitated, and the wave rose over her and was gone.

Andi was nearby, turned in the other direction. Cassie sure hoped no one saw her bail like that.

Then she spotted a figure in the distance, another surfer she hadn't noticed before. The figure started paddling closer. It was Micah.

Of course. *Why does he catch me in all these embarrassing situations?* she thought. *So not fair.*

And of course her heart was beating-beating-beating as he approached. She tried to calm it, not sure why this kept happening whenever he was even remotely nearby.

"Hey," he said. He came up beside her and took a seat on his blue board.

"Hey," she choked out. He made her feel so not-herself, so strange. She looked out at the sky instead of at him. But the sun was coming up bright and hot and she couldn't look straight at it or else she'd go blind. So she *had* to look at him. She just had to. That's what she told herself, anyway.

"Have fun last night?" he asked.

"Yeah," she said. She could have probably continued this conversation all in monosyllables without even trying.

"You seem pretty popular already," he said.

"What?" If he meant everyone attacking her for quitting the surf team, that's not exactly what she'd call popular.

"I meant with Charlie and Ben," he said. Then he caught the look on her face. "That was a stupid thing to say," he added.

"I don't like them if that's what you're asking. Is that what you're asking?"

"No."

"Oh, okay. Never mind then."

The lapping of the water was all that could be

heard. For one tiny second, Cassie wanted the ocean to swallow her.

"Actually, yeah," Micah said, "I guess I was just going to warn you about Ben. If you had a thing for him, I mean."

"I don't."

"Then I guess I don't need to warn you . . . Not that you seem like someone who couldn't take care of herself."

"Thanks," she said quietly.

She stretched out on her stomach so she could dip her arms in the water. It was strange to just dangle there in the ocean, after what had happened. But she kept still. She willed herself not to start seeing shadows in the blue-green abyss below, not to freak out. See? She was perfectly fine out here. No worries. None at all.

"So Ben's a player, huh?" she said a little too loudly, trying to keep her mind off all the water below and around her in every possible direction, everywhere.

"You didn't hear it from me," Micah said.

She put her cheek to the board and turned to look at him and not down into the water. He was on his stomach now, too, stretched out on his board. She met his eyes and held them. They were deep brown, so deep she couldn't pull away even if she tried.

Cassie wanted to ask him if *he* was a player. Someone as cute as he was . . . he had to be, right? But she couldn't ask that. She didn't know why she cared anyway. It's not like she liked him—she wasn't the kind of girl to fall for a boy so fast. It had never happened before and it probably never would.

Weird, though, that she couldn't keep her heart in check when she looked at him.

Just then, a good wave came down the pipeline, straight for them. Micah motioned toward it and kept back, as if to say, *It's all yours.*

But she shook her head, and put a hand to her rib cage as if she had a swimming cramp. "Go for it," she called to him over the rush. And he did. And while he was up on it—he had good form, riding it hard—she took the opportunity to paddle out of the deep water, back to shore.

That first week, as a swimming C.I.T., Cassie

was helping the counselors with the campers' swimming qualifications. There were two swimming counselors—Alexis, with close-cropped hair that was dyed pale blond, and who was so good of a swimmer that word was she'd almost gone to the Olympics, and Lucas, a dead ringer for Adam Brody, who was coaching the campers to leap off the diving board into the huge Camp Ohana pool.

Cassie's fellow swimming C.I.T., Neil, wasn't much of a talker. This Thursday, all he'd said so far to Cassie was the usual aloha. She could see him across the gigantic pool, in the shallow end, showing the butterfly stroke to some beginning swimmers. Cassie was working with the sprinters in the deep end.

Cassie used to hate pools—she didn't understand the concept of them when the ocean was right there, filled with all the water you'd ever need. But this week she'd been perfectly content to spend time in the pool, rather than out in the endless ocean just steps away. There was something about the pool's contained rectangular shape, its blue-painted walls, the fact that it *had* walls . . . that just made her want to stay afloat inside.

Of course, the swimming counselors had other

things in mind. "Hey, Cassie," Lucas called, "we need one more stopwatch so we can time the laps for the swimming qualifications—could you ask Haydee, the surf counselor, if she has an extra?"

Cassie turned toward the ocean, searching for Haydee. The surfing counselor's distinctive pink-streaked ponytail could be spotted at once, far away from shore, bobbing up and down in the waves. She was out in the deep waters, sitting astride her surfboard with some campers from the surfing class gathered around.

Seeing how far out they were, Cassie mumbled, "Can't, uh, Neil go ask?"

Lucas gave her an odd look. "Just swim out there, okay? No rush, just see if she has an extra."

"Sure," Cassie said. What else could she tell the counselor? *Hi, I know I'm supposed to, like, know all about swimming and stuff, but I'm scared of the ocean, so could I hang out in the chlorine instead?* And it wasn't even as if she was scared of the ocean. More like if she could avoid it, she would.

So she did it quick. She ran across the beach and waded into the waves. As she did she caught sight of a group of boys nearby—aged ten or eleven. They were huddled together on their boards, splashing, laughing. Danica, their surfing C.I.T., was there, too, coasting on her surfboard. Cassie wasn't being paranoid . . . but it did sort of appear that they were looking in her direction.

"Shark!"

Cassie froze. Did they say that for real or was she hearing things?

"Help! Shark!" She was sure she heard it that time. When they saw her looking, they burst into laughter, giving them away. Danica covered her mouth to keep from laughing. She looked straight at Cassie, as if this was a joke all on her.

The boys were just kids. Cassie didn't know whether to blame them or Danica.

"Just kidding," one of the boys yelled to Cassie. But they were still cracking up.

"Not funny," she called back.

"Oh, don't take it so hard," Danica called. "It was just a joke." She paddled over to Cassie. "Can't you take a joke?" Danica said.

Cassie was determined not to show what she was really feeling. She forced herself to act blasé. "People shouldn't really yell shark in the ocean," she said, trying to sound matter-of-fact. "It's like basic surfing ethics."

"And you would know all about that, I suppose," Danica said. "Seeing as you're a pro and I'm not."

Cassie fumbled for a response. Danica had a way of catching her off-guard, making her even more unsure of herself than she already was.

Haydee paddled up on her surfboard at that moment. "Tell me you didn't have anything to do with that, Danica." Nearby, the boys were being whisked out of the water—it looked like they were being punished.

Cassie felt numb. And stupid, really stupid. There was also this big part of her that wanted to just get out of the water, and fast.

"Did you?" Haydee said to Danica.

Danica took a moment—Cassie wondered if she'd lie—then said, "It was a *joke*."

"You should know better," Haydee said coldly. She did not look happy.

"Um, Haydee?" Cassie interrupted.

Danica's eyes held Cassie's, a questioning look on her face. *She thinks I'm going to defend her,* Cassie realized.

But what Cassie said was, "Haydee, you don't have an extra stopwatch so we can time the swimmers, do you? Lucas asked me to ask you."

"Sure, take mine," Haydee said, giving Cassie the waterproof watch hanging from around her own neck.

Cassie could just feel Danica staring daggers at her as she waded to the shore.

She didn't have to swim far out into the ocean, but still, Cassie decided to take this opportunity for a short break. Lucas *did* say it wasn't a rush. She could see Tori on the sand, lounging on a beach towel. As a camper, Tori had a ton of activities to go to that Cassie wasn't a part of, so they didn't get to see as much of each other as they'd hoped—but this afternoon happened to be Tori's swim activity. In fact, she was supposed to be in the pool getting ready for the swim qualifications at that very moment. Instead, she was lying on her back, *ELLEgirl* magazine forming a tent of shade over her face.

Cassie ran up and kicked her leg to wake her. "Tor, do you want to do the swim test now? I'll time you."

From under *ELLEgirl* came a groan. Then a mumbled response: "I'm reading."

"Where are the rest of the *pinaos*?" Cassie asked about her bunkmates.

Tori lifted an arm and lazily pointed toward the pool. "I told them I'd meet up later. I'll take the swim test when they make me. You're not coming over here to make me, are you?"

"No, but I should," Cassie said. Then, to show just how serious she was, she sprawled out on the sand beside her cousin, resting her head on the corner of the towel beside Tori's. "You do know how to swim, don't you?" she teased.

"Of *course*," Tori said.

"Then what's the deal? You get in the pool. You kick and paddle, kick and paddle. You reach the end, I tell you your time. That's it."

Tori wasn't paying attention. A boy from her division was coming out of the ocean, his hair wet and dripping down his face, his eyes on Tori. "Hey, Tor," he said as he passed her towel, still dripping.

"Hey, Eddie," she said.

A look was shared between them and then the whole interaction was over.

Tori relaxed again on the towel, a blissful smile on her face.

"Who was that?" Cassie said.

"My boyfriend twenty-four hours into the future," Tori said, smile widening.

"*What?*"

"That's Ed, from California. I call him Eddie. In one day, two at *most*, he'll be my boyfriend," Tori said, like she could predict the future.

"Who *are* you?" Cassie cried. "Where do you get that confidence? Is it from this?" Cassie shook the *ELLEgirl*, like some kind of magical romantic wisdom would fall out on the sand. Instead, a subscription card dropped out.

Tori patted the sand for her Dior sunglasses, then set them on her nose. "I dunno. I know he likes me, and I like him, so what's the drama? We'll see what happens."

Cassie shook her head. "If dealing with guys was that easy, I'd have had a boyfriend by now." Then she stood up and tried to pull Tori to her feet. She was sure that the swim counselors were most definitely noticing how long she was taking to get the stopwatch.

But Tori wouldn't budge. "I'm not up for a swim right now, k?"

Cassie put a serious look on her face. "These aren't sympathy pains, are they?"

Tori met her eyes for a long moment before bursting out laughing. "What, like, we're so totally connected, so if you avoid the ocean I do, too?"

Cassie nodded.

"No, I'm not afraid of the water, Cass," Tori said with all seriousness. "I just don't feel like being all sporty today. I want to chillax on the sand with my sun and my fashion mag. And here I thought being *related* to the swim C.I.T. would get me out of these lame tests. Not happening, huh?"

"Not forever," Cassie said. "You know, it's a wonder we get along at all. You hate sports; I love sports. You love fashion; I wouldn't know a Mike Jacobs original if it fell out of the sky and landed on my head. How are we even related?"

"*Marc* Jacobs," Tori said from behind her glasses. "And you like Marc Jacobs—remember that shirt I let you borrow the other night? That was a Marc Jacobs."

Cassie didn't answer. Now she was a little distracted.

"Remember?" Tori said. "Cass, what're you looking at?"

Cassie, had she the words to tell her cousin, would have explained what, or rather who, she had her eyes on. But there were no words. She'd forgotten the concept of words.

Micah had walked up and was now standing beside her. She couldn't seem to remember having such a thing as a tongue.

Micah spoke for her. "I said hey," he said. "And hey there, Tori, how's it going?"

Tori sat up. Cassie could see her taking in the whole deal: Micah being friendly, Cassie turning to stone. Then he was gone, with a wave. And Cassie could breathe again.

"What just happened?" Tori said. She pulled Cassie back down to the sand with her. "Did you have a mini-stroke or something?" She felt Cassie's forehead and cheeks. "Do you have malaria?"

Finally Cassie found a word. "No," she said. "I was trying to figure out what to say to him and I couldn't think of anything and I just clammed up, I guess."

"You guess? You guess!" Tori shook her head.

"Wow, Cass, I had no idea you were so completely socially inept with boys. This is, like, way more serious than I ever realized."

Cassie let out an incoherent shriek and put her head in her hands. "It's not that bad," she mumbled. "I just feel so funny when I see him. Like I can't catch my breath or something—it's so weird."

"Cass, that's what *happens*," Tori said gently, "when you *like* someone."

Cassie tried to deny it. "No, I think I'm just stressed out."

"Haven't you ever liked someone before, like, really liked someone?"

Cassie gazed blankly at Tori.

"Oh. My. God," was all Tori said.

Cassie sat up and looked around the beach. She spotted Micah across the sand, talking to Danica. Danica seemed pretty upset, probably due to the whole shark incident in the water. It looked like Micah was maybe trying to comfort her. He had his hand on her arm. She had her head on his shoulder. Oh. Now they were hugging.

Tori had seen it, too. "Oh, yeah, and then there's that," she said in a low voice.

"I didn't know they were so . . . what's the word . . . familiar," Cassie said slowly. She was feeling a new weird thing now, a shivery falling feeling, like her guts were about to spill out all over the sand. She looked away.

"Well, sure," Tori said quietly. "Of course they're familiar."

"What do you mean?"

"They were together last summer," Tori explained gently. "When they were both campers here."

"No," Cassie said.

"Yes," Tori said.

Cassie hung her head. It didn't make sense why something like that—something *in the past*—would matter so much to her, but it mattered, it did.

"Don't be so upset," Tori said. "It's obviously over. Look how he's standing, keeping some distance from her? He's so over her, obvs. Nothing to worry about, see?"

"Okay," Cassie said, trying to see this, though she couldn't see it at all. "And I'm not upset."

"Whatevs," Tori said with a wink, clearly trying to lighten the mood.

"I'm not," Cassie insisted.

A shrill whistle sounded out from the direction of the pool. Seeing a quite possibly angry swimming counselor waving at her to bring over the stopwatch, Cassie shot up. "Whoops, gotta go," she said. And she bounded off, relieved to have somewhere to be, something to do, other than sit on the sand and wonder what was up with Danica and Micah.

I don't care, Cassie told herself. Still, as she hustled back to the pool, she knew it would take a lot of convincing.

Five

On Friday, the surfing C.I.T.s were giving beginning surfing lessons to the younger campers. Micah remembered being a beginner well. When his family had moved from St. Louis, he'd figured surfing would be a lot like skateboarding: Just remove the wheels and substitute water for pavement beneath your feet. But there was more to it than that, and his first wipeout proved that. When he'd been learning to surf, he didn't take lessons. There was no counselor-in-training—no anyone—to teach him what to do. He'd had to figure it out for himself. And now here he was teaching kids.

"But I can't stand up!" Abby, one of the campers in Micah's group, was complaining. She was belly down on one of the camp's white surfboards, her hands gripping the sides so tightly, her knuckles were the same color as the board. She wasn't even making an attempt to stand up.

The youngest group of kids at Camp Ohana were age nine. Abby wasn't even one of the youngest: She was eleven. The surf counselors, Zeke and Haydee, had pretty much given up on her and left her in the C.I.T.s' hands. Which meant that Micah and Danica, the other surfing C.I.T., would be the two to help her at least make a passable trip on a surfboard one time before leaving the island for the summer. But Danica wasn't handling it so well. Poor Abby was miserable. Her face had gone puffy like she'd burst into tears.

"She'll never get in the water," Danica said dramatically to Micah. "Never."

Working with his ex-girlfriend for the summer may not have been what he signed up for, but Micah had a way of putting aside the things he didn't want to think about. He wasn't going to make a big issue about it, no matter how awkward it felt, no matter how hurt he'd been when they broke up. He wasn't going to dwell on the past.

"She'll get it," Micah insisted.

"Take her to the sand," Danica said. "She can practice standing up on the board out there."

One of the surf counselors, Haydee, overheard this and nodded. "Good idea," she called over. "Reviewing the basics couldn't hurt."

So Micah pushed Abby's board—with Abby clutching the edges with all her might—to the shore. Once on the sand, she loosened up a bit and no longer seemed about to cry. With the white surfboard face up on the sand, Micah had Abby practice starting on her belly and jumping up to a squat.

From his spot on the sand, he could see Danica and the counselors continuing with the surf lessons. Some of the beginners were making real progress. He saw a nine-year-old from New Jersey take a wave and ride it halfway down the beach, a little shaky, but still impressive for the first time. He waved at her and she shrieked in excitement.

"You must think I'm such a loser," Abby said to Micah. She was flat on her stomach and had stopped even trying to practice the squats.

He crouched down to talk to her. "I don't, not at all," he insisted. "It just takes some getting used to, being out on the water."

"But *you*—I bet it came easy for you."

"You want to know what happened my first

time out? I fell flat on my back and my board landed on top of me, like this . . ." He mimed the disaster, probably looking like a downed crab. "It's a miracle I didn't drown."

"No!" Abby said, cracking up. "You're just saying that to make me feel better."

"Oh, I'm serious," Micah said. "I wouldn't lie about that."

When he stood up, brushing sand off his back, he saw Cassie looking his way. Their eyes met and then—as if she'd touched poison ivy—her gaze slapped back in the total opposite direction.

"You want to try the water again?" he called down to Abby. "Right there at the shore, by the tides?"

"You'll stay with me?" she prompted. She looked up at him with big brown eyes.

"I'll stay with you," he assured her, "until you catch your first wave and start surfing without me."

"Okay," she said reluctantly. They carried the board out to the very edge of the ocean. Micah let it float and nodded to let her know she should take her place on it. She did, gripping it tightly on the sides. But that's all she did. She was frozen again.

Haydee waded up and smiled down at Abby. "How's it going?" she said.

"I'm getting there," Abby piped up. "I'll get up on this thing before the end of the summer, I swear."

Haydee patted Micah on the shoulder and then caught sight of Cassie in the distance. "Abby, now look over there. Have you met Cassie? Do you know she won the under-eighteen North Shore contest her first time out? And I bet her first time surfing was a struggle, too."

Abby looked out toward Cassie. So, of course, did Micah.

Cassie and her swimming group seemed to be finishing up. Whistles were blown and they headed out of the water. Cassie started wading toward shore. As she did, Haydee waved her over.

"Cassie, this here's Abby. She's about to take her first wave today. Any advice?"

Cassie smiled at Abby. "Just have fun," she said. "I used to forget that when I was surfing, but that's always the most important thing."

Micah saw the look in her eyes—a flash of sadness maybe. Then it was gone.

"See?" Haydee said to Abby. "Once you loosen up and have fun, you'll be thrashing these waves in no time. Plus, you have an awesome teacher."

"Micah *is* a good teacher," Abby said.

"I have an idea," Haydee said. "Cassie, how's about you join us? You're not officially a surfing C.I.T., but you're always welcome to join our activities, I hope you know that."

"Oh no, it's okay," Cassie said. "Micah and Danica have got it covered."

"The offer's open," Haydee said. Then she caught sight of one of the campers nose-riding a wave without falling off. The boy was balanced on the front end of the surfboard—the nose—while it rushed forward on the motion of the wave. "Go!" Haydee cried. And she swam back to help the other kids get on the boards.

Micah and Cassie stood there awkwardly, with Abby on the board between them. "I should really go," Cassie said. "I'm not a surfing C.I.T., so—"

"No one cares about that," he said.

"No, really, I should go," she said. She took a few steps toward shore.

"It's hard to have fun," Abby said at that

moment. "When you're scared you're gonna drown, I mean."

Cassie stopped and turned. "You won't drown," she said to Abby. "Especially not with Micah here helping you."

Abby braved a smile. "Yeah," she said.

Then Cassie seemed to change her mind. "But I could help, too. If Micah doesn't mind."

"I don't mind," he said. "Abby, we'll get you up on that board in no time."

Abby grinned.

"You know what I used to do?" Cassie said. "I'd try to stand with my eyes closed. Just the standing part. It sounds crazy, I know, but that's when you think you're gonna fall. Once you're up on the board it's like you're flying."

"Really?" Abby said. She looked from Cassie to Micah, then back to Cassie again.

"Yeah, really," Micah said.

It took some convincing, but soon, with her eyes closed and Cassie and Micah each holding one of her hands, she was able to jump up to her knees. They let go and she even rode a wave that way, opening her eyes halfway. "It *is* like flying!" she cried.

114

"We'll get you standing in no time," Cassie said.

"I don't know . . ." Abby said.

"Don't be scared," Cassie said. "The waves are good today. It'll be an easy ride."

Abby was now sitting upright on the board, floating in the water. But sitting was better than lying down—it was a huge improvement and a big start. "What's the worst thing that ever happened to you?" Abby asked Cassie. "I mean when you were surfing."

Cassie met Micah's eyes. He wasn't sure how much she'd say.

"I had a big scare once," she said. "It was really nothing." Here she looked at Micah, as if daring him to fill in the details. He didn't. "Only, I was scared after. Really scared. Like something awful happened. It's still freaky to think of going out there." She stopped talking then, as if she'd confessed too much. She was watching the waves in the distance, the ones too far out for anyone to be riding.

"Really?" Abby said. "*You* were scared?"

"Anyone can get scared," Cassie said. "Maybe it would help me out if you showed me how it's done."

She gave the water a splash and smiled at Abby. "Nothing to it, right?"

Abby laughed, but there was a look of determination on her face, like she wanted to show both Micah and Cassie that she could do this before the day was over.

Abby made more attempts to leap up on the board. She went for a few small waves, didn't catch any, but she'd certainly loosened up—which could only help. And then there was the moment when Abby found herself on her feet, coasting toward shore. Sure, the water was only knee-deep, the wave she was riding was barely a ripple, but she was doing it. Both Cassie and Micah whooped in encouragement.

"I did it! I did it!" Abby cried. One of her friends approached her on the beach and she hopped off to do a full reenactment of her first big wave.

"Impressive," Micah said to Cassie, once they were alone. "Too bad you're not one of the surfing C.I.T.s. You're good at this."

"Oh, I didn't do anything," Cassie said. "You were the one teaching her all morning. Besides, Danica's the girls' surfing C.I.T. No worries." There was something in her voice that made Micah see she wouldn't fight for it. There was also something in the way she said *Danica*, like she had done it only to get his reaction.

They gazed at each other for a long moment. All around, were kids splashing and laughing and completely not paying attention to the fact that the two of them were standing there with nothing to say.

"Anyway," Micah said, breaking the silence, "you're good with the kids."

Cassie opened her mouth, about to say something, when Danica paddled up on a surfboard. She sandwiched the board between Cassie and Micah and stopped.

"What was that about?" Danica said, nodding toward Abby onshore.

"Did you see?" Cassie said with obvious delight on her face. "Did you see her take that wave? It was awesome!"

"I saw," Danica said. "I saw you teaching the class when you're not even the C.I.T. here. What, you think me and Micah can't handle it? You think just because you're supposedly some big pro you can splash around here, taking over my job?"

"*Danica,*" Micah said. He couldn't figure out

her problem with Cassie. It was like having another surfer around made her think she had to have a throwdown.

"I was just talking to her," Cassie mumbled. "No big."

"No big? No big!" Danica's green eyes were blazing. Micah had never seen her act this way before. "I know you think you're the best thing since *ever*, Cassie, but if I get a shot at that inter-camp surf contest in Oahu, I'm going to show everyone that I can win. What'll you think about that then, huh?"

"What surf contest in Oahu?" Cassie said.

"The huge, gigantic competition with all the camps all over Hawaii surfing against each other?" Danica said loudly, like Cassie was dumb.

Cassie shrugged. She had no idea there was even a contest in Oahu.

This seemed to enrage Danica even further.

"Danica, chill about the contest," Micah said. "Haydee said Cassie could help out with the surf lessons if she wanted. And Cassie's good with kids. We should thank her. Did you see Abby ride that wave?"

"I *said* I saw," Danica said.

A sharp scream pierced the area.

All three C.I.T.s turned in alarm to see where it was coming from. On the beach, a girl from Cassie's swimming class was crying hysterically, holding her foot.

"Oh no," Cassie said in a low voice.

"Yeah, you're great with kids, Cassie," Danica said. "The one who's screaming isn't one of *my* campers—she's yours."

But Cassie didn't hear that last comment because she was running toward the girl. So was Emmy, the lifeguard on duty. Micah started over, but Danica pulled him back.

"You like her, don't you?" Danica said.

"Who?"

"Don't play dumb. Cassie, who else?"

"What do you care? You broke up with me almost a year ago."

"About that . . ." Danica started. But before she could finish, Emmy was calling out to everyone on the beach that the girl had only cut her foot on a shell. The horror-movie screaming was over and the girl had graduated to pouting now. Micah could see Cassie helping the girl to her feet, letting her lean on her shoulder.

"I should go help. She's probably taking the girl to the infirmary," Micah said.

"Whatever for?" Danica said. "The kid can hop on one foot, can't she?"

A whistle blew and the surfing activity was over. The C.I.T.s were to gather the kids in the group and herd them back toward the beach, then clean up.

After all the kids were safely out of the water, the two surfing counselors approached Danica and Micah. "We've got some news," Haydee said.

Zeke cleared his throat like he was about to speak. He was usually the quiet one of the pair, but he seemed almost animated at this piece of news. "This'll get you stoked," he said. "Ohana's having the surfing expo early this year."

Micah recalled the expo from last year and how all the C.I.T.s and counselors practiced their surf skills like mad, hoping to impress the judges. Everyone said the contest was rigged—the guy who won the top surf prize was the guy who had always won the top surf prize. But he wasn't here anymore—he was too old to be a C.I.T., and he hadn't come back to be a counselor. That meant the top prize was wide open. Micah had to go for it this summer.

"How early?" Danica was saying. "I don't get much practice in at home in Florida during the year—the summertime, when I'm here at camp, that's my only real time to surf. You guys know I need time to practice before the big contest. This is my first shot to win it." She was acting like the whole thing was a setup only for her.

"Well, it's been moved up," Haydee said. "We've got some pro surfers coming to judge both the boys' and girls' contests and their schedules made it so they couldn't come at the end of the summer . . . You won't believe what the prize is."

"We're stoked," Zeke said. "But we're not telling."

"So *when* is it?" Danica repeated.

"Next weekend," Haydee said. "On Visiting Day."

Danica let out a huge sigh and rolled her eyes.

"What, you're not stoked?" Zeke said.

"Dude, why does everything have to make me stoked?" Danica snapped.

"Are you stoked?" Zeke said, an eyebrow raised at Micah.

"Yeah," Micah said. "I'm up for it."

Zeke nodded, apparently satisfied at his stokedness. "Just wait'll you kids see the prizes, you'll be—"

"Stoked. I get it, Zeke," Danica said.

Zeke shrugged. "Just sayin'," he said.

Micah had never heard Zeke say so much in one sitting.

"Danica," Haydee said, "what's up with you? This is a great opportunity. The prize is killer. You've had this attitude all week—this is not the Danica I know."

Danica's face softened a moment. She met Micah's eyes. "I *am* stoked," she said quietly. "I just want that first prize. I want it more than anything, you have no idea."

"That's the Danica I remember," Haydee said. "Because if this attitude is some problem with the two of you working together, I don't want to hear it. I don't care if you're broken up or not. None of that matters out in the water."

Danica shrugged. "I've got no problem with Micah," she said.

"Haydee, seriously, me and Danica working together is no issue," Micah said.

"Good."

"So only surfing C.I.T.s and counselors can compete, right?" Danica said suddenly.

"What, the two of you? No, *all* C.I.T.s can compete. Speaking of . . ."

Micah could see Danica's face getting pinched.

"Where's that surfer chick? I want to give her fair warning about the competition. She's up for a fight." Haydee winked at Danica.

"You mean Cassie?" Micah said. Danica looked like she might bite his head off at the mention of her name. "She took one of her kids to the infirmary."

"Anyway, she shouldn't be allowed to enter. She's pro," Danica said, clearly hating having to admit that out loud.

"Any C.I.T. can enter," Haydee said. "Besides, it sort of racks up the competition, no? Gets your blood flowing. Makes you want to win?"

"Oh, I'll win," Danica vowed. "Then I'll go to Oahu and take that contest there . . . if we get a shot at it. Will we, Haydee? Will our camp be sending surfers to compete in the Oahu contest?"

Haydee had a small smile on her face. "Not telling. Anyway, that's the attitude I like to see. You'll give Cassie the news about next weekend, yeah?"

"We'll tell her," Danica said.

Haydee grinned. "But first, clean up these boards." She nodded at the scattered white surfboards left on the sand where the kids had abandoned them. Then she took off for the rec hall, leaving them to deal with the mess.

Danica had her own ideas. "You'll handle this, won't you, boo?" she asked Micah. "I have *got* to tell Sasha and Sierra the news."

"Danica, I'm not cleaning this up without you."

"Then don't clean it up," she said. Soon she, too, had taken off down the beach. Micah was left to clean, sort, and carry the boards back to the stands. If only boys could compete against girls in that expo: Ex-girlfriend or not, Danica would get a run for her money.

Micah was putting the last of the camp boards away, but this time he took the long route around the back of the showers, knowing he'd cross near the infirmary. *Maybe Cassie will still be in there,* he thought.

And what do you know, there she was, walking out.

"Hey," he said as if he just happened to bump into her. But there was no reason to act shifty: He actually had news to tell her, about the expo.

"Hi," she said. She seemed more relaxed around him now—*finally.* "So Tamra cut her foot up pretty bad, poor kid. She was just walking on the sand and stepped wrong on the shell and . . . Anyway, she's on the phone with her mom."

"That sucks," he said. "But I'm glad I ran into you," he said. "Haydee and Zeke wanted me to tell you some news about the surf contest. You know all about that, right?"

"Yeah, sure," she said. "There's some kind of contest in August, right?"

She was so nonchalant about it—he figured she just knew she'd win. With skills like she had, a little contest like this was in the bag. He wished he had her confidence. And more, he wished he had her skills.

"They moved it up—the whole expo's moved up . . . to Visiting Day this weekend."

"That's cool," she said. "So you're competing in it, right?"

"Yeah, of course. You are, too, right?"

"Oh, I don't know yet," she said vaguely. "I thought I'd have more time to decide, you know . . ." She wouldn't look at him. Now she was back again to not looking at him.

"I just figured . . ." he started. "But I guess because of the . . . I mean, I guess it makes sense that you don't know if you'll do it."

"What are you doing with a board all the way over here?" she asked, clearly wanting to change the subject. "Don't they get put away on the other side of the beach?"

"Yeah," he said. It wasn't like he could explain how he took a detour to the infirmary so he could have this non-conversation with her and make a fool of himself.

"Huh," she said. He had no idea what *that* meant.

"You should compete," he shot out. "You'd be awesome. I know a week isn't long enough to get over whatever you need to get over but . . ." Here he stopped. "Anyway."

Her eyes darkened. She looked about to burst out with something, but someone came running up shouting her name. It was her cousin, Tori. She shrieked and leaped into Cassie's arms. Micah took a big step back.

"Eddie asked me!" she cried. "We're hanging after dinner tonight. I knew it! Did I say I knew it or did I say I knew it?!"

"You knew it," Cassie said, this huge smile on her face.

"Sorry to interrupt," Tori said to him, "but Cass and me, we've got to talk."

"Yeah, sure," he said, and backed away with the board.

He tried not to look over his shoulder to see if Cassie was watching him go. He tried not to, but as he turned the corner, he did look.

And there she was, standing with her cousin, talking animatedly. She wasn't looking in his direction, not at all, like she'd forgotten he'd ever been there.

Danica went looking for Sierra and Sasha everywhere. They weren't in the C.I.T. bunk, not on the beach, not in the pool, not in the rec hall. She wanted to tell them about how the surfing expo got pushed up weeks ahead of time. *It's all so I don't get good enough to beat Cassie,* she suspected. *They want Cassie to win, so they're making sure she does.*

Danica wanted someone to complain to, and she knew Sierra and Sasha would listen. Only Sierra and Sasha weren't anywhere she could see. By the time she found them—just walking the pebbled paths, chatting like they had nowhere to be—she was so riled up, she wasn't able to explain it properly.

"I don't get it," Sierra said, after Danica had told her about the expo now happening on Visiting Day, "are your parents coming and you don't want them to see?"

"My parents?" Danica said. "No, they never come for Visiting Day—it's too far and they're too busy. This has nothing to do with my parents."

Sasha spoke up. "And you still get to surf in the contest, right?"

Danica sighed. "Yeah, of course. It's just that

Cassie . . ." she said, trying to find the words. "Cassie is all—" She stopped talking then. Sierra and Sasha turned to see where she was looking, which was at the path outside the infirmary where Cassie, the very person she'd just mentioned, was standing with Micah. They couldn't seem to stay away from each other, apparently.

"Are they together now?" Sierra said.

Danica didn't answer.

"If they are . . ." Sasha started. "Danica, that sucks."

"But Danica doesn't like Micah anymore, right, D?" Sierra said quickly.

And then Danica's two best camp friends were looking right at her, waiting for confirmation that she was so far over Micah that she didn't care who he was crushing on, but they didn't get anything of the sort. Something on her face gave it away.

"You do still like him!" Sierra said.

"She *does*," affirmed Sasha, eyes wide.

"Just shut up, okay?" Danica said. They were talking pretty loudly—she didn't want Micah and Cassie to overhear. "And by the way, they're not together. It's nothing . . . they're just talking."

"They're not together," Sierra said, studying them from afar, "not yet."

Sasha put an arm around Danica's shoulders. "Don't worry, D. It'll never happen. Micah will *never* like someone else. Not with you here."

"Yeah!" said Sierra.

"Yeah," Danica said. Her voice was very small, barely recognizable as hers. It was bad enough she had to deal with the drama of Cassie stealing her *extremely deserved* spotlight just by being at Ohana this summer, but now Cassie was going after Micah, too? That could not happen. It just couldn't.

Six

There was another Camp Ohana C.I.T. tradition in the works, and this one had to be kept top secret from campers and counselors alike: night swimming.

Every summer, the C.I.T.s and some of the lifeguards snuck out after lights-out to go swimming. Tonight's swim was planned for the usual cove on the beach, just a five-minute walk from camp grounds. The girls in the C.I.T. bunk were getting dressed for the night out when Andi came up and sat on the end of Cassie's bed. "I'm wearing black," she said. "So if I blend in with the dark and you can't find me, just call my name and I'll come running."

"Okay," Cassie said. She had to admit: Andi made more of an effort with her than the others girls. Cassie couldn't say for sure, but it almost seemed as if Andi wanted to be her friend.

"So, this place we're going, the counselors won't hear us there?" Cassie asked.

Andi shrugged. "Well, they could hear, I guess. It is pretty close by."

"Why aren't we going to one of the saltwater lagoons?" Cassie said. "I used to go to this one place close by a lot when I was a kid—just with my family, before I started traveling so much. It's called Lani Kohola . . ." Cassie stopped talking. She wondered if she should have brought it up. This tradition had been in place for years. But Cassie still was reluctant to go swimming in the ocean at night, and she knew that the only real safe spot to swim at night was an enclosed lagoon, something smaller than, well, the expanse of the *entire ocean*.

But Emmy, who had also grown up in Kona, knew the exact spot Cassie had mentioned. "Guys, we have to go to Lani Kohola. It's this little lagoon you can't see from the road, it's *gorgeous*. Great idea, Cassie."

"No, really, never mind," Cassie said. "It's actually not a good idea. It's a *local* spot."

This got Danica's attention. "Yeah, so?"

"I mean it's for locals only. Only locals go swimming there. No tourists."

"We're not tourists," Danica said.

"I didn't say you were a tourist," Cassie began, fumbling. "I just meant you don't live on the island—most of the C.I.T.s aren't from here—so we shouldn't really go. I really shouldn't have brought it up."

"What would happen?" Andi piped up. "I mean if we all went swimming there and, you know, some locals showed up to swim there, too."

"Oh, nothin' will happen," Emmy said. "I know everyone. Everyone knows me. If any locals come by, I just say hey, dudes, it's me, Emmy. No worries."

"So it's decided then," Danica said. "Lani Kohola it is."

Cassie should have kept her mouth shut. Emmy acted like it was no big deal to bring a bunch of strange kids to a secret spot used only by locals, but Cassie wasn't so sure. Locals in Hawaii were known to be *very* protective of their secret spots. Everyone's heard a story of a tourist who got banged up by a local just for dipping his toe in the wrong stretch of beach. But Emmy was acting like such a thing wouldn't ever happen with her around, so Cassie shrugged it off.

But then she got nervous when the guys said the best way to get to Lani Kohola would be to swipe one of the Ohana vans for the short ride. Somehow she was now complicit in grand theft auto—and all she'd wanted was somewhere calm to go swimming!

Cassie was going over her anxieties—one more was that she wouldn't be able to string together a coherent sentence now that Micah was around—when she got a welcome sight: her cousin Tori, running across the sand in a bathing suit.

"I snuck out!" she whispered when she reached Cassie. "So did Eddie." And sure enough, Tori's new boyfriend emerged from the shadows, along with one of his friends. They hopped in the Ohana van with the C.I.T.s and the lifeguards—jam-packed in the back—and were soon at the lagoon.

Lani Kohola, the saltwater lagoon hidden from view of the road, was a shimmering green pool in the night. The air smelled wonderful—a touch of this incredible sweetness that Cassie recalled from her childhood.

It didn't take long before Cassie forgot her stress. Tori helped, but it wasn't just her cousin who was

134

making sure to include her. Andi was, too. Shortly into the evening, Andi had motioned to Cassie to come join her group.

Me? Cassie thought at first, surprised.

Soon, Cassie found herself in the midst of it, covering her face from the splashes. All around her the other C.I.T.s and the lifeguards whooped it up, but she didn't feel as separate from them as she usually did. She was here, with them, a part of this just as much as anybody else.

Tori swam over and they floated together at the edge of the lagoon on their backs, looking up through the ring of palm trees at the stars.

"You havin' fun?" Tori asked.

"I'm glad you came," Cassie said. "I just hope you don't get in trouble for it."

"I won't," Tori said confidentially. "But yeah, I'm glad I came. Did you *see* Eddie?"

"Tor!"

"Just kidding, Cass. I'm glad I'm here. I get the feeling you need me."

Flashlights skittered on the shore above, showing Ben approaching the hill overlooking the lagoon, about to jump in. The group screamed in encouragement. Cassie and Tori swam off to the side, giving him room, but when Ben hit the water, a giant wave still cascaded up to their chins. He'd gone in feet-first but somehow tipped over and landed in a classic belly flop, splashing everywhere.

"Owwwww!" Ben moaned when he surfaced at last.

Some girls were cracking up. Danica was laughing, standing on the sand in a bright turquoise bikini, pointing at him. Cassie noticed that the only girl who wasn't in some form of hysterics was Emmy. She was looking at Ben with this serious expression on her face, as if concerned that he'd hurt himself. Tori saw, too, and swam closer to Cassie to whisper in her ear.

"Look who likes Ben!"

"No," Cassie said, somewhat in horror. "She can't think he's cute, can she?"

"Well, technically, he is cute, like, on paper. But in person, he's sort of . . ." Tori treaded water, searching for the word.

"Obnoxious?"

"Yeah. Just like Charlie is cute, technically, on paper, but when you talk to him, he's, like, too awkward to stay cute, you know? It sorts of cancels it out."

"He is too cute!"

"Wait, you don't like him, do you?"

"No."

"I know who you like!" Tori shrieked. Cassie could see her cousin's smile in the darkness. She could see it, and she knew the name that would cross her lips next. She just didn't want it said out loud, not here where anyone could hear.

She leaped toward Tori, covering her mouth so the name couldn't come out. "Shhh!" she cried.

"What are you guys talking about?" said a voice. Andi swam up. "What's the secret? Tell! Tell!"

"It's nothing," Cassie said. "Totally and completely absolutely nothing."

"You're talking about boys," Andi said. "I knew it."

At this, someone else swam up, but in the dim light Cassie couldn't make out who it was at first. Cassie's stomach sunk when she realized it was Danica. "What boy?" Danica said. "You have to tell me. Don't think I won't find out."

"No boy!" Cassie protested. "Really."

Tori was thankfully silent, though she knew very well the exact boy Cassie was not thinking of at that moment. He was on the hill overlooking the water. He was calling out to watch out below. Then he was diving in. Cassie watched him make a smooth impact, then turned away before he surfaced.

"Good," Danica said, "because this is no time to be thinking about boys. What with the contest coming up. I just hope Cassie's ready for it."

Cassie stopped floating and stood again in the water, surprised to be called out.

"Yeah, you heard me," Danica said. In the dark it was hard to tell if she was being serious or not. "It's gonna be tough. I'm pretty good. You probably didn't know that, but I am. Ask anyone here. And I happen to know you're out of practice. Didn't you say you haven't been on a board in, like, forever?"

"I'll be okay," Cassie said.

Tori stepped up to defend her, as always. "Oh, she'll rock it," she told Danica. "You can be sure about that."

"Really?" Danica said.

"Yes, really," Tori shot back.

Cassie didn't know what else to say. Fact is,

Danica had a good point. No matter how good Cassie had been in the past, she hadn't surfed in months. Was it like riding a bicycle, like once you learn how to thrash waves your body never forgets? She had no idea, and now Danica was using that doubt to psych her out.

Tori waited until Danica had swam away and was toweling off onshore with her friends, then said, "What is her *problem*?"

"Oh, that's Danica," Andi said. "She's just like that. You get used to it."

"Like what? *Mean*?"

"She takes Ohana really seriously—she loves this place. And you, Cassie, you're new." She shrugged. "Anyways, you have nothing to worry about in that surf contest. I mean, obviously you'll win."

A huge splash came from nearby and Andi tried to duck it. It caught her on the head and she shrieked. "You're dead, you are so dead!" And then she was paddling for Charlie, trying to get back at him.

Cassie stood there in the water practically up to her neck, not saying anything.

"You *will* win, Cass. You know that, right?" Tori said quietly.

"I'm getting out," Cassie said. "I'm done swimming." She headed fast for shore. On the sand, she searched out her towel and dried off. Tori quietly joined her.

"Cassie?" someone said.

She turned to find Micah. She didn't remember seeing him leave the lagoon after he dove in off the hill, but there he stood, dried off, his T-shirt on.

"You want to take a walk?" he said. "Just down the beach and back?"

Cassie fiddled with her bag, looking for something she didn't even need. What did that mean, a walk on the beach? Where would they walk? What would they talk about? What should she say? There were too many questions and not enough answers. Before she even realized what she was saying, the words came out of her mouth: "Nah. Thanks, though."

Micah didn't seem to expect that answer. "Uh, yeah, you're welcome," he said. Then they looked at each other, as best they could in the dim light, sort of dazed.

Can I put my head in the bag now? Pretend this isn't happening? Cassie wondered. She could not believe she had actually told him no.

Then Tori came to the rescue—as always.

"What she means is yeah," Tori piped up. "We're dying for a walk. Aren't we, Eddie?"

Eddie had just shuffled over and was standing there as confused as Cassie. "We are?" he said.

"Yeah, we so are," Tori said. She pushed Cassie forward, a step closer to Micah. "Right, Cass?"

"Yeah, sorry," Cassie mumbled. "I got confused."

In a matter of minutes, the four of them were on a long stretch of beach, the sound of splashing and laughter echoing in the distance. Tori and Eddie held hands, walking with their toes in the lapping tides. Cassie and Micah walked silently side by side, enough space between them that their hands never touched. Cassie wondered what would happen—what stupid thing would shoot out of her mouth—if they did.

"This isn't about the surf contest, is it?" she finally asked. It was the only thing she could think of, and she was desperate to break the silence.

"No," he said. "I was just wondering what you were doing this Sunday."

"Why?"

"Just, Sunday's our day off . . ."

She walked blankly through the darkness.

When she'd look back on this moment, she'd want to smack herself upside the head. "On Sunday?" she said. "I guess I'm doing laundry."

Laundry?!

"Oh," he said. "Cool."

"I need to get detergent," she said.

"Yeah, you'll need that."

"But it can't be Tide." He was silent for a moment, so she continued. "Tide gives me hives."

"It does?"

"I guess it's really strong stuff or something. I get these huge red welts, they itch like crazy and—Um. It's just gross."

In her mind was an incoherent wordless thought of only: *????*

Truly, she had no words for the fool she was making of herself.

"That's too bad," he said.

"That I'm doing laundry?"

"No, I mean I was gonna say you could borrow some of my detergent, but I think maybe it's Tide. So . . ."

"So then I shouldn't, you know, 'cause that would be like really . . ."

"Gross."

"Yeah."

"Yeah." They'd reached a turn in the beach. "I guess we should head back now," he said.

"Okay," she said.

It was the most meaningless conversation she'd ever had.

But then Micah stopped. She felt so out of sorts, she wouldn't have been surprised if hives had spouted up all over her face. "You really have to do laundry on Sunday?" he asked.

Tori and Eddie were passing by at that moment. Tori stopped and inserted herself in the conversation. "She's not doing anything on Sunday," she said. "Why, are you guys going out somewhere?"

She was asking like it had already happened. Like Cassie hadn't just mortified herself over laundry soap.

"I was thinking we could take a drive off camp grounds," Micah said. "Sunday morning."

"That sounds like fun. Right, Cass?" Tori poked her hard with an elbow.

"Uh-huh," Cassie said.

"She'll be there," Tori said.

But Micah was looking at Cassie for the answer. He seemed to want to hear it from her own lips. "You sure?" he said. "You have time with all that laundry?"

"Sure," she said. "Laundry can wait. I'll be there."

Danica was enjoying her swim in the lagoon— even with Cassie around. Danica was doing perfectly fine, diving in, splashing with her girls, gazing up at the stars, loving this island that she only got to see in the summer, hearing people calling her name from all directions, everyone always calling her name, wanting her to be a part of things, as it should be . . . when she realized some people were not in the lagoon with everybody else.

Cassie.

And Micah.

She stopped swimming and looked around for them. The water reached to just under her neck. She had her arms down at her sides, down in the warm water, so it hid her hands, which were balling up into fists where no one could see them.

"What's up?" Sasha asked her.

"Nothing," Danica said. Even if her friends did know she was into Micah again, she didn't want it to be a public topic of conversation. She should never have admitted it in front of them, not until she was sure Micah liked her back.

It was at this moment that Tori and Eddie, and Micah and Cassie, ambled up. They must have wandered away where people couldn't see them. Talking about her, probably. Danica was sure of it. They'd gone out of her earshot to talk about her, only because she'd had a few words with Cassie about the surf contest.

What's the big deal? Danica thought. *I can try to psych out my competition if I want to. That's like* expected.

But then she saw how close Cassie and Micah were talking. Were they holding hands? It was too dark to see for sure. Suddenly, she felt a sense of uncertainty in her gut, a bottomless insecure feeling she wasn't used to.

Sasha saw where Danica was looking. "Uh-oh," she said in a low voice. "Cassie moves fast."

Danica felt on edge, exposed, like everyone

knew her business and they were all laughing about it behind her back, as she would, if it were anyone else.

"Just go talk to him," Sasha said. "He'll totally want to get back together with you. I mean *totally*. Cassie doesn't stand a chance."

Danica wanted to ask her friend how she could be so confident. Was it really that much of a given that he liked her again, especially after what she did last summer? Micah had walked away from Cassie now. He was talking to the guys, just standing there, looking like his usual cute self, completely oblivious to Danica's change of heart.

"You're gonna go talk to him, aren't you?" Sasha said. "This is the perfect moment."

"I'll wait till he comes to me," Danica said. *Obvs.*

Micah looked up and saw the two girls watching him. Danica had a flash of gratitude that she'd worn her turquoise bikini, seeing as she looked so good in it. Then he started walking over—she saw it for sure, the first few steps—and then she saw him stop short when the bright lights were shining through the palm trees.

Everyone stopped what they were doing. There was a mad scramble as the C.I.T.s and lifeguards left the lagoon and scattered for the van. Danica realized she was the one who had the van keys so she took off running, too. In a matter of seconds, it seemed, all the C.I.T.s and lifeguards were safely piled into the van and they hit the road. The bright lights were headlights, just as suspected, but no one could determine what the car was. It didn't matter, really, just as long as they got out of there and back to the Ohana campgrounds before anyone knew they'd been gone.

No problem, it seemed.

Danica, seeing as she somehow found herself with the van keys, ended up at the wheel. She let off most of the C.I.T.s and lifeguards at a side entrance into the camp, so the big group could sneak back to the bunks as quietly as possible. Then she pulled the van around to the lot and parked it where they'd found it. Sasha and Sierra had stayed with her, and they all carefully crept from the van, closing the doors with the faintest of clicks. All they had to do was return the van keys to the hook in the C.I.T. director's office and—

"Danica!"

The sharp voice cut across the sandy lot, hitting Danica flat in the back. She knew that voice without even having to turn around.

It was Simona, the C.I.T. director. "Danica, *what* are you doing?"

Danica froze, but Sierra and Sasha—her two most loyal friends on the island—jetted off in opposite directions, leaving her to deal with the fallout on her own. And of course, the incriminating evidence was in her left hand, jingling there like a beating heart. With the keys to the van in her possession, she couldn't deny a thing.

Danica sat in Simona's office, on a green wicker chair that poked sharp sticks in her thighs. She still had on only the turquoise bikini, but now she was far less grateful to be wearing it. Now she felt ridiculous. Also, she felt cold. And queasy. And a little annoyed at her friends for leaving her to take all the blame. Now, whenever she wore this turquoise bikini, she would forever remember this moment with the stabs of the wicker and Simona looking all disappointed and that particular shade of blue her knees turned when she was cold because she had bad circulation. She'd never be able to get over this, would she? The bikini was effectively ruined forever, and that, somehow, seemed like the worst thing of all. She used to love this bikini.

All she could see out the windows was the dark night, just this flat blackness without any sight of stars. The ocean roared in the near distance, ferocious. And Simona paced, just as ferocious, before Danica's green wicker chair.

Danica had never seen this side of Simona. Okay, Simona was a big girl to begin with. She was tall, and broad-shouldered, and let's just say you would not want to be behind her in the pool if she was kicking. She was not someone you wanted to make mad.

"Danica, you realize I have every right to call the police right now and have you arrested," Simona said.

You wouldn't, Danica thought in horror. What she said instead was only, "Please don't . . ."

Simona nodded. She sat. The wicker chair she

chose sunk beneath her in crackles and pops and Danica forced herself to keep a straight face. "I'm not calling the police, Danica. I just wanted you to realize how serious this is. Do you?"

"I do," Danica parroted back. Where was everybody else? Why was she the only one of the whole group of C.I.T.s and lifeguards to have to suffer through this lecture? Could the woman at least throw her a blanket so she didn't have to sit here shivering in her bikini?

"I hope you do. I could send you home for this," Simona said.

"Home!" *That* got Danica sitting up in alarm. In fact she sat up so fast, she got a wicker sword in her leg that could have poked a major artery. "Simona, please. I'm sorry. I was borrowing the van, just to, you know, go for a drive, I don't know, get some fresh air, it was stupid, I should have never done it, I know that, but please don't send me home."

Simona kept all trace of expression from her face. *She wants me to think she'll send me packing,* Danica realized. She could not get sent home early.

Then again, she wouldn't rat out her friends here to stop that either.

Now Simona was leaning forward and trying out this friendly tell-me-everything smile, saying, "Let's talk about who was with you. I know you didn't take that van alone, Danica." She stared hard at Danica, willing her to spill.

Danica had this picture in her mind of a girl with a yellow surfboard and light brown hair: Cassie. All she had to say was Cassie's name. And it wasn't even a lie—Cassie had been there. It had been her idea to go to Lani Kohola, after all.

But even Danica couldn't do that. She just shook her head.

"You're not going to tell me, are you?" Simona said.

"It was all me," Danica said.

Simona shrugged. "You can try to be as honorable as you want . . . you're still in trouble." And this was how Danica learned she wouldn't be able to take part in the expo. And if there was another strike against her—if she did just one more thing wrong—then she would lose her position as a C.I.T. and be sent home.

As Danica walked back to the *nai'a* bunk, taking her time through the pebble-covered paths, she let herself breathe in the ocean air.

She lost her shot at winning that expo—and she so would have won, bet on that—and it was doubtful that the counselors would send her to the big inter-camp surfing contest in Oahu now, but at least she could stay. She could stay! And, for a moment, that felt good enough.

Then her mind turned to Cassie, who would probably win and take Danica's spot, not to mention Danica's boyfriend. Danica couldn't bear the thought. She couldn't let Cassie have *everything*.

Seven

Cassie could barely sleep Saturday night, knowing she'd be waking up before breakfast to meet Micah. She tossed, she turned, and by the time she crawled out of bed, she was so anxious and sleep-deprived, she worried she wouldn't look cute enough for her date with Micah. Or rather, her maybe-date— she wasn't even positive it was a date. Who goes on a date at seven A.M. on a Sunday morning? Cassie had never heard of such a thing.

Immediately she thought of Tori. Tori would know. *I wish I could talk to her,* Cassie found herself thinking as she got dressed and dug out her flip-flops from under her bed. Then, as if by magic, Cassie caught sight of Tori out the bunk window, dragging a giant bag between the hammocks.

Cassie figured Tori must have gotten up early,

too, to wish Cassie good luck and maybe give her a second opinion on her outfit. But when she ran out to meet Tori, who had stalled and was heaving, trying to catch her breath, Cassie quickly learned that this wasn't the case.

"I'm on laundry duty," Tori said, shooting a look of pure hatred at the laundry bag in question that was bulging with sheets and towels. "My counselor, Lauren, caught me sneaking back in last night. So this is my punishment."

"No!" Cassie said. Then she clamped a hand over her mouth because she realized how loudly she'd said it. Where they stood between the hammocks was close enough to the *n'aia* bunk to be heard and wake up all the C.I.T.s.

"Lauren's making you do laundry this early?" Cassie asked.

Tori shoved out her lower lip in a pout. "It's cruel and unusual punishment to force someone like me to get up before eight o'clock on a weekend—I should call Amnesty International. And, besides, do you know how grody my bunk's dirty towels are? I could get scabies!"

They looked at each other in horror.

Cassie snapped out of it and grabbed the other end of the laundry bag, to help Tori with the weight. "Let me help you get this to the laundry room." She couldn't help but feel responsible. Whose idea was it to go to that lagoon off-campus, anyway? Hers.

But Tori pulled the laundry bag away. "Don't touch!" she hissed. "You'll get that cute shirt dirty."

"Who cares?" Cassie said. "Let me help, seriously."

"Get your hands off my moldy laundry, Cass, *I'm* serious. You have to go meet Micah, like, right now. And, by the way, you look adorable. Blue's your best color."

Cassie smiled nervously, all her massive insecurities rearing their many heads yet again. "You don't think I look like I'm trying too hard?"

Tori smiled. "You look like you. And he likes *you*. So go! Before he thinks you stood him up."

Cassie tried to protest, but her cousin insisted. She looked back one last time at poor Tori fighting the whale of a laundry bag across the sand. But then, in the distance, she saw Micah standing beside a beat-up old Jeep in a bright white T-shirt and black shorts. All at once, she felt like she'd heard you're supposed to when you see someone you really like—that heart-skipping-a-beat cliché, it actually happened in real life!

Even if this wasn't technically a "date," it sure felt like one. Especially when she stepped up to him and said, "Hi." And he said, "Hi," and there was only that—those two words—and the breeze off the ocean and the sun in their eyes. If that moment could have expanded to fill up a whole entire day, she would have been happy.

"So," Micah said at last, "are you up for a drive?"

"I didn't know you had a car here," she said, though she was standing beside it.

"My dad's old Jeep, yeah. He gave it to me when I got my license. It gets around okay . . . that's all I need it for."

"Yeah," she said.

"Do you have a car here?"

"I don't have my license yet. I'm sixteen, but I just, you know, haven't gotten around to it."

"Right, because you travel so much."

She nodded. "I used to." She didn't want to talk about what she used to do, so she changed the subject. "So where are we headed today?"

"It's a surprise," he said.

She hopped in the Jeep and soon they were headed down the back roads of the island, out a ways from Kona, toward she didn't know where, and she didn't really care. She just liked sitting next to him, the wind whipping through her hair as they drove.

It wasn't until they pulled off onto a narrow sand-covered road that she began to get an idea of where they were headed. She saw the bright blue-green ocean sparkling through the gaps in the palms. He was taking her surfing. *Of course.*

She should have realized. *How much more obvious could it be?* she thought.

It was early in the morning—the best time to go surfing; any surfer knew that. And—she could see through the rearview mirror—there were two surfboards stacked in the back of the Jeep. People from Hawaii always kept boards stowed in their cars, sure, but somehow she knew that one of the two boards back there was meant for her. Coincidentally, she was even dressed for surfing—she always wore a bathing suit under her clothes, that was normal growing up here, like people on the mainland probably walked around all day wearing underwear. She was ready to go surfing, as if this had been the plan all along.

Micah probably assumed she'd known from the beginning. He wouldn't have specified Sunday *morning* if he hadn't been trying to give her a hint.

If this had been a date, he would have asked me to go out at night, Cassie realized. She felt stupid for not realizing this earlier.

The Jeep pulled to a stop in a bank of sand. "Surprise!" Micah said. "I heard about this spot from the surf counselors and thought we'd check it out. What do you think? The surf report this morning said there'd be some pretty good height." He gazed out at the waves—and they were a good height, just as promised. "Lookin' good," he said.

Cassie felt utterly disappointed. She felt dumb, dumb, dumb.

"Cool," she said weakly. "I didn't actually realize that's what we'd be doing today," she added, "surfing . . ."

Micah had already jumped out of the Jeep and was pulling the boards onto the sand. "Uh, yeah," he said, seeming confused. "Isn't that what we were talking about last night?"

"I thought—" Cassie started. But she couldn't say what she'd thought.

Micah dropped the second board on the sand and stood it upright to lean on it. The sun washed over him, showing off the contrast of his white shirt and his cocoa skin, his curly hair moving in the breeze. But his eyes, deep brown and intense, settled on her, seeming worried. "Didn't you think that's where we were going this morning?" he said carefully.

"You said it was a secret," she said lamely.

Micah circled the front of the Jeep, coming around to open her door for her. She hadn't left her seat. "I was thinking it would . . . I don't know . . . maybe get you comfortable again. With surfing. You know, in time for the expo next week."

He was holding the door open for her so she could jump out. It took her some seconds to do so— and there was this big part of her that didn't want to make the jump. This part of her that wanted to stay in the Jeep. To make him turn around and take her back to camp. Going surfing was so not what she wanted to happen on her maybe-date.

What did I want to happen? she thought wildly. *A romantic picnic on the sand? With chocolate-covered strawberries and a ukulele playing in the background?!*

It was ridiculous. Micah clearly saw her as one of the guys—just someone to go surfing with—and she should have known that.

Normally, this would have been no problem, no problem at all. She'd surfed with guys and girls alike; she'd been known to go up against the big waves with anybody, it didn't matter who, or when, or where. But that was the old Cassie, the Cassie who never would have spent the summer at Camp Ohana in the first place. The person she was now still did not want to go out on that board.

She didn't want Micah to see that, though.

So she stepped out of the Jeep. She shrugged her shoulders, as nonchalantly as she could muster. "Cool," she said. "Which board's mine?"

"I guess I should've told you," he said. "In case you wanted to bring your own board. I was thinking maybe you'd show up with it."

"It doesn't matter," she said. She was acting cold, but she couldn't help herself. That's just what was coming out of her when she thought of surfing the waters this morning—coldness. She felt frozen inside.

They were wading out in the water when it all went wrong. All of a sudden, Cassie could see ahead to what would happen: She'd get on the board, belly down. Micah would do the same on his board. The sun would beat down on their backs. Then a wave would come—a good wave, no, a *great* wave. It would wash straight toward them, begging for a ride, and Micah would of course let her have it. So she'd feel like she'd have to try for it, of course. She'd feel pressured, forced to make herself do it. And she'd try to jump up, try to push forward and stand, but then something would happen. Something always did. And she wouldn't be able to stand up. The wave would pass her by. She'd make a fool of herself in front of Micah again, she knew it.

It felt like her fate was already predetermined.

You know what? she thought suddenly. *I'm not gonna let it happen.*

So all at once she started wading back to shore. She rushed out, and it wasn't till she stood with her two feet out on dry land that she felt any better.

Micah stood confused in the waist-deep water. "What are you doing?" he called.

"I'm not up for it," she called back. "I'm

just—" She shrugged. "I just don't want to surf, okay?"

He started wading out, pushing the board in front of him. "Yeah, okay," he said. Then they stood awkwardly together on the sand.

Cassie didn't know what to say. She'd ruined the whole morning, she'd ruined everything, and she should have thought to keep her mouth shut, because it was about to get much worse. "I just, you know, don't want to, okay?" It came out sounding defensive.

"I said okay," Micah said. "You don't want to, no worries, you don't have to."

"Good," Cassie said.

"I didn't realize it was such a big deal," Micah said. "What happened. You know, with the—" He paused. "The shark."

This was just how her surfing coach and her surfing teammates had responded—taking her alone out to surf, thinking getting back in slowly would make all the difference, would get her to forget she almost got herself chewed up by a shark. Maybe other people could forget something like that, but Cassie was having a hard time doing it.

So sue me, she thought. *I can't help how I feel.*

What she wanted to say to Micah was how mortifying it was to be unable to face up to your fears. Some days she was okay; other days she wasn't. She wanted to explain that to him, to say: *Sorry. I am so, so sorry this turned out to be a not-okay day.* But those words would not find their way to her lips.

Instead, she said, "It's not a big deal. I'm over it. I'm just not into practicing for that expo, that's all— that contest is just not something I'm interested in."

WHAT did I just say to him?

Then her mouth kept on going: "It's just some little contest," she said. "For amateurs. I stopped doing that kind of thing when I was, like, twelve."

He just looked at her. "You know what," he said at last, "I heard you. I get it. The contest next week's not a big deal to you. Fine, whatever. It's a big deal to me, though. So let's just drop it, okay?"

"Fine. Considered it dropped."

"Great."

"Good."

"We should go," Cassie said. "Besides, it looks like it might rain."

They both glanced up at the sky. Cassie was relieved to have something else to look at besides his face or her own feet—and she figured Micah felt the same way.

"Yeah, I guess we should," Micah said.

The drive was too awkward for words. Cassie kept herself turned toward the window, watching the side of the road as they made their way back to Ohana. The plastic top of the Jeep was pulled up, and rain began to drum down as they were halfway back to campus, loud enough so there was no point to talking. That, Cassie realized, was her first bit of good luck all day.

The rain turned heavy. By the night, Cassie was holed up in the bunk, feeling sorry for herself and worse for Micah—who obviously had meant no harm. She'd tried writing him a letter multiple times, but after many scribbles and cross-outs, all she had worthy of showing him was:

I'm an idiot. I'm sorry for what I said. Can we forget what happened and start over?

"It's *awful*," she heard from across the bunk. "It's, like, the absolute worst thing that could have happened, like, ever."

"I know. It's just wrong. Like, so wrong."

Cassie bolted up in her bed, hid the page she was attempting to write, and looked over. Her two fellow C.I.T.s Sierra and Sasha were talking with wide gestures. *Did they hear about what happened with Micah?* Cassie thought in a panic. She hadn't expected the news of how terribly she'd treated him to travel so quickly—now people were even talking about it with her in the room!

Sierra saw her looking. "Don't *you* think it was just awful?" she said pointedly.

Cassie realized that she was alone in the bunk with Sierra and Sasha. Rain poured outside. A storm like this was unusual in Kona—this part of Big Island was known for its always pleasant weather. Rain, any rain, was rare, and a storm like this was especially strange to see. It fit Cassie's mood perfectly.

"Well, don't you?" Sierra repeated.

"I—" Cassie started.

"*Poor* Danica," Sasha said.

"What do you mean?" Cassie said. *Maybe they*

*don't know what happened with me and Micah.
Because what would Danica have to do with it?*

Wait . . . does *Danica have something to do
with it?*

She was totally confused.

"What, you don't know?" Sasha asked. She
turned to Sierra. "She doesn't know!" At this, they
scrambled over to Cassie's bed to fill her in on the
Danica gossip and how she got caught red-handed
with the van keys and got banned from the surf
contest next weekend. The strange thing was, even
though Danica could have shared the rap with all the
other C.I.T.s and lifeguards—it's not like she snuck
out on her own—she hadn't ratted a single other
person out. She'd taken the fall herself.

Sierra and Sasha were shaking their heads,
repeating again and again how this was the worst
news ever, but Cassie did notice that they seemed to
love talking about it. When another C.I.T. entered the
bunk, they repeated the exact same news to her.

Cassie left the bunk and stood out on
the lanai. Sheets of rain fell on all sides—she
couldn't even see out to the other bunks. The
humuhumunukunukuapua'a bunk was just across

166

the way—Micah could have been inside, maybe—but through the dark night and the rain she couldn't see.

Again, she felt somewhat responsible—she'd been the one to first mention Lani Kohola. Maybe if she hadn't said anything, all the C.I.T.s would have gone swimming as usual in the Camp Ohana stretch of ocean, and no one would have gotten in trouble. More importantly, Danica would still be competing on Sunday.

Cassie stared out into the pouring rain. She felt bad for Danica, she really did. And the worst part was that there wasn't anything Cassie could say to her that would make a difference.

"Isn't this storm awesome?!" Andi shouted, interrupting Cassie's thoughts as she ran up the bunk stairs.

Cassie shrugged. She wasn't a fan of rain—when it was raining, you couldn't surf. Not that she planned on surfing; she was just used to seeing rain as bad news.

"Hey, did you hear what happened with Danica? She can't compete in the surf contest," Andi said. "That means you'll win for sure."

"I heard," Cassie said. She didn't mention that

she didn't want to compete. She also didn't mention that, more importantly, if she *was* competing she would definitely want Danica in the contest with her. If Danica was a good surfer, the contest could only be better if she was surfing in it.

"Hey, you haven't seen her around, have you?" Cassie asked.

"I think across the way, on the lanai of the *humuhumunukunukuapua'a* bunk," Andi said, pointing into the dark rain. "Here, if you're going out there, take my umbrella. You'll get drenched in two seconds flat." She left her dripping umbrella in Cassie's hands and went inside.

Cassie took a step toward the rain, then she hesitated. Danica wouldn't want to talk to her. And, besides, what was she doing at Micah's bunk? Something about that didn't feel right. Before Cassie could wrap her brain around it, though, Danica herself shot out of the rain and onto the lanai where Cassie was standing. She shook herself out and then the umbrella, clearly drenched from wherever she'd been.

Cassie tried to think of something to say. What she wanted to do was apologize for what happened, to ask if there was anything she could do. What she said instead was, "Wet out there, huh?"

Danica lifted her head, gathering her long hair into a wet, messy bun. "Clearly," she said, like Cassie was dim.

"Danica . . ." Cassie started.

"Yeah?" Danica said. She had her hand on the door knob, ready to go inside.

"I, uh, I heard about what happened with Simona . . . and the expo."

"Yeah, *and*?"

"Well, that sucks and I just wanted to say I'm sorry," Cassie said quickly.

"You're sorry . . . whatever for? Because it was your idea to go to that lagoon? I didn't tell Simona, if that's what you're worried about."

"I'm not. I know you didn't tell. I just feel bad that you can't compete."

"You and me both. Because as I said, I would've killed it."

They held each other's gazes for a long moment.

"Yeah, well, I'm going inside," Danica said. She slipped in and let the door slam behind her.

Maybe I should say something to Simona, Cassie thought, standing alone out on the lanai. Then she took it back. She'd be crazy to help someone who was always so mean.

Eight

The rain had stopped by Monday morning, but that didn't mean the ocean was safe for swimming. Micah noticed the red flag hanging off the lifeguard tower on the Ohana stretch of beach. That meant violent surf—no swimming or anything else—until further notice. For the rest of the day, the water was off-limits.

But the Camp Ohana staff had plans in place for bad weather. The campers wouldn't have to sit bored stiff in the rec hall all day, playing checkers and making friendship bracelets. A hiking trip to a nearby park called the Hau'oli Lava Caves was swiftly organized.

As Micah and the other C.I.T.s and junior counselors helped pack the vans with supplies, he found himself still dazed from his trip with Cassie the previous morning. How stupid was it to assume she'd want to go surfing after all she'd been through? He wanted to say something to her now, but he didn't know how to begin the conversation.

There she was in the other van, loading a cooler into the back with Andi. Andi waved with her free arm, but Cassie didn't wave. He looked away. He was relieved when they ended up in different vans on the way to the caves.

The Hau'oli Lava Caves (or "Happy" Lava Caves, as the name translated from the Hawaiian) were a series of inactive lava tubes open to tourists, spelunkers, and explorers. The tour guide, a short bald man in khaki hiking gear, had gathered the campers outside the entrance to the caves to give them some history on the place before they were free to wander around inside. Micah was the C.I.T. assigned to watch over the *mo'o* (meaning "lizard" in Hawaiian) bunk, a group of twelve-year-old boys who could barely stand still let alone listen to what the tour guide was saying.

"Hawaii Island, otherwise known as Big Island because obviously it's the biggest of all the islands making up the great state of Hawaii, was formed from five separate volcanoes," the tour guide explained. "Only two volcanoes are still active. The caves that make up our park aren't caves at all. They're really a series of lava tubes from one of those volcanoes. The tubes you're about to explore are said to be more than a thousand years old, so in fact—"

"C'mon already! Let's just go in the volcano!" yelled one of the boys from the *mo'o* group.

"Fine, fine, just put on your helmets and go on in the caves. But don't be too loud in there—or else you'll cause an eruption," the guide said. He had a frazzled, serious look on his face, so it was hard to tell for sure if he was teasing.

Micah knew he had to be, but the boys in his group heard the word *eruption* and stopped shouting for a moment.

"He's kidding," Micah assured them. But maybe he shouldn't have said that, because as soon as they knew there was no danger they stormed down into the cool, craggy darkness of the caves and resumed shouting.

Micah led his group through the ancient tunnels—or his group led him. At one point, one of the boys did a running leap off a stalactite and came sprawling straight at Micah. They skidded in the dirt and both fell.

"C'mon, guys," Micah said from the ground. "Tone it down a few notches. For me."

All was well—he hadn't broken anything—until Micah caught sight of Cassie around the crooked bend of one of the tunnels. The warm glow of the dim lights strung throughout the caves made the place seem almost red, as if still filled with lava. He saw her wandering past, a flash of her beautiful hair and her adorable walk, and he awkwardly got back on his feet. He thought to lead his group after hers, to instigate a collision, so he and Cassie could maybe have a few words, but then, in another tunnel across the way, he caught a glimpse of Danica. She was laughing and having a blast with her group. And after he'd heard Danica was asking after him at his bunk the previous night, he wondered if maybe he should head off to have a few words with her.

He was torn between the two tunnels, the two girls.

But there was no time to make a choice between one or the other because the *mo'o* bunk was terrorizing the tour guide around the bend.

Micah did the responsible thing like any good C.I.T. and jetted off after them. If Danica wanted to talk to him, she'd find him later. Same went for Cassie—if she ever found the heart to talk to him again in this lifetime, she knew where to find him. Just follow the screaming *mo'o* bunkers; that's where he'd be.

Meanwhile, Cassie was the C.I.T. assigned to the *pinao* bunk—Tori's bunk—as she'd been hoping. She followed the winding lava tubes, putting her hands against the cool hardened walls, trying to pretend to have a good time. The air was filled with a red glow, like they'd wandered onto some other planet. To be deep inside an actual volcano . . . it was almost too symbolic. Cassie felt about to burst, too.

But thank the volcano gods for Tori, Cassie thought. Because every lava tube they entered seemed to have Micah just coming out of it with his group. Or walking past. Or going in.

Once, they met halfway inside a slim, dark passage—he was going one way, Cassie was going the other—and they exchanged these words:

"Hey."

"Hey."

"You're standing on my foot."

"Oh sorry."

"Don't worry about it."

"Okay, see you later."

"Later."

And that was that. After witnessing this awkward exchange, Tori grabbed Cassie and pulled her away from the rest of the *pinao* bunk to have a chat. "You haven't talked to him since Sunday morning?!" Tori asked incredulously. Of course, Cassie had recounted the disaster later, but maybe Tori didn't understand the depths to which Cassie had sunk. The fool she'd made of herself. The awful awfulness of it. No wonder all that she and Micah could say to each other was that one was standing on the other's foot. (For the record, *Cassie* had been standing on Micah's foot— just one more strike against her.)

"No," Cassie admitted to Tori. "I can't talk to him. It's too weird."

"Because you're madly in love with him," Tori said.

Of course, the other girls in the *pinao* bunk

overheard and soon they were all crowded around Cassie, wanting to know who she loved madly, and did he love her, too, and were they gonna get married (squeals, shudders, boos, hisses), and had they kissed yet, and on and on and on. Soon, the whole thing became a blast of loud gibberish and the Hau'oli Lava tour guide came by and told them to shush.

"I am not in love with him!" Cassie protested after the tour guide left.

"But you like him," Tori insisted.

"No," Cassie said. Then, "I don't know."

"Who?" someone said. Entering the tube was another group, the headlights on their helmets turned up so high it was almost blinding. Danica was behind one set of lights, Sierra behind another.

"Who do you like?" Sierra repeated.

"Nobody," Cassie said.

"Uh-huh," Sierra said in a loud voice, as if she knew the answer already. She turned to Tori. "So your boyfriend's cute."

Tori smiled blissfully. "Yeah, have you seen him?"

"Down the tubes thatta way. What's his name again?"

While this conversation was going on, Cassie and Danica lowered their headlights and met eyes. "How are you doing?" Cassie said quietly. She was still feeling awful for Danica.

"I'm fine. Why wouldn't I be?" Danica said, eyes narrowing.

"I don't know, I was just asking."

"Don't feel sorry for me, I'm fine," Danica said.

Cassie didn't want to move and accidentally step on Danica's foot—so she stood up against the wall, waiting until Danica finally lost interest and left.

When Danica, Sierra, and the campers headed for another tunnel, Tori turned to Cassie with big eyes. "*What* was that about?"

"What?"

"You know what! Acting like some groupie in front of Danica. Who is she, Nicole Richie?"

"No, I just—" Cassie looked around. The *pinao* girls were exploring deep in the bend of a lava tube where she couldn't see them. She'd hate to be the C.I.T. who lost a camper, thanks to her own personal drama. "Maybe we shouldn't talk about this now," she said. "Besides, someone might hear."

Just as she said these words Cassie caught sight of Simona. She stood alone in a nearby lava tunnel, appearing to study the cracks and fissures in the walls. Simona was either very, very interested in old rocks, or she was wandering around checking up on her C.I.T.s. In fact, if Simona came any closer, she'd be able to hear what Cassie and Tori were saying. She'd be able to hear *everything*.

That's when Cassie had the idea.

"Just tell me what's up," Tori was saying. "The Cassie I know would not kiss Danica's butt for no reason. You're scaring me right now. You're scaring me more than the idea of this volcano exploding while we're in it. Spill."

Cassie felt like maybe fate had tunneled down into the volcano to save her. The truth is, she didn't want to surf in the expo. She didn't want to surf at all! Didn't anyone *get* that?

"It's my fault," Cassie spilled, raising her voice. She spoke loud enough so that anyone nearby could hear. "Danica got in trouble, even though sneaking out to Lani Kohola was all my idea."

"What-*ever*," Tori said.

"And you got in trouble, too," Cassie continued.

"And that's my fault. No one seems to think I had anything to do with it, but you know Danica can't compete in the expo because of this, right? Because of me." There. She'd said it. Any second now Simona would mosey on over and . . .

Tori kept talking. Her back was to Simona and she had no idea. "You are, like, totally self-centered if you think this is all about you. And I'm not mad at you, so don't even go there. I snuck out on my own time."

Cassie shook her head. She wanted the focus back on Danica, not Tori. She couldn't let her cousin get in even more trouble! "But Danica really wanted to be in that surf contest. Like, *really wanted* it. If she can't compete, then I shouldn't get to either. I should tell the counselors. Or Simona. It's not fair."

"Cass, you're crazy," Tori said. "You can't tell, I won't let you!" In her excitement she whipped around and that's when she saw Simona. The expression on her face changed in a flash—from serious and concerned to wide-eyed and maybe a little scared. The tinged red light of the lava tubes didn't help the effect.

"I think the damage is already done, Tori,"

Simona said. Standing before them, she seemed even more imposing than usual, so tall she completely blocked the way out of the tunnel.

"Uh, um, uh-oh," Tori mumbled.

"Hi, Simona," Cassie said quietly. Now that it was out, she could barely talk.

Simona patted Cassie's shoulder with a heavy hand. "You, me, and Danica," she said. "We'll talk about this later, back at camp." Then she headed off, disappearing into a dark tube.

Cassie found her voice. "She's never going to let me surf now," she said.

Tori took a long moment, studying Cassie like they were in a court of law. "You saw her there, didn't you?" Cassie didn't answer so Tori continued. "This is what you wanted the whole time, isn't it? You wanted something to happen so you wouldn't have to compete." She didn't seem angry, just sad.

Cassie shrugged. Instead of answering, she tugged on Tori's arm. "C'mon," she said. "Let's just get out of this volcano."

When Cassie and her group emerged from the lava tunnels, she caught sight of Danica leaning up against the outer cave wall. She wasn't alone, but her usual hangers-on, Sasha and Sierra, weren't with her. Micah was. Cassie tried her best not to notice Danica whispering something into Micah's ear, or Micah letting her. She tried not to notice how Danica had her mouth out, her eyes closed, as if about to kiss him. She especially tried not to notice whether Micah kissed back or not—so she turned her back on the whole scene and just stood there a moment, feeling like a tool.

How could I have thought for one second that he'd asked me on a date?!

Obviously he liked Danica. Obviously.

Tori came up and rested her chin on Cassie's shoulder. She just hugged her for a long moment. "That sucks," she said. Cassie knew she meant Micah and Danica. "I guess they're getting back together," she added quietly.

"Yeah," Cassie said. "I don't care."

"Okay," Tori said.

"Really," Cassie tried to insist. "I said I don't care."

"And I said okay," Tori said.

Cassie hugged Tori back. She cared, oh how she cared. She cared so much that she didn't know if she could move from where she stood, not for many minutes, not ever again. Seeing Danica and Micah together like that hurt in a way she'd never felt before. If she'd known that letting herself like a boy could turn itself into *this*, she wouldn't have allowed it to happen. She would never have looked at him. She would never have gone on that walk with him. She would never have talked to him or taken that drive with him or . . . anything. She would never have let him even enter her thoughts.

Then again, when it came to Micah, she suspected she wouldn't have been able to stop herself had she tried.

Micah stood with Danica outside the caverns. She'd led him over to the wall, wanting to talk, to tell him something or other, but he didn't even know what because as soon as he'd leaned in to hear it, she'd pulled his face close for a kiss.

He'd pulled back in shock—he wasn't expecting it, is all.

And now they were fighting over it. Just like old times.

"You like her, don't you?" Danica said, eyes blazing in the direction of one of the Camp Ohana vans.

"Who?" Micah said, playing dumb. (He could see Cassie climbing into the van with her cousin out of the corner of his eye.) "Seriously, Danica, what's your deal? First you break up with me then you try to kiss me. What am I supposed to think?"

Danica huffed out a huge sigh. "I had a moment of weakness. I must've gotten lightheaded from the lava tunnels, obviously. Forget this ever happened." She pulled far away from him. Then she put up a hand to wave. "Hey, Ben!" she called.

Ben waved back.

"You don't like Ben," Micah said in a low voice. Then he had a moment of doubt. "Do you?"

"Why?" Danica said with a smile. "Jealous much?"

Micah was about to deny that accusation, of course—he wasn't jealous. No way, no how, not a cent. And yet. Maybe he didn't know how he'd feel if she got together with someone else this summer.

Still, before he could come up with a suitable response, Haydee, one of the surf counselors, came bounding up. She grabbed Danica and pulled her into a hug. "You might be back on!" she cried.

"Back on what?" Danica said.

"Back in the contest this weekend. I was just talking to Simona, and she said she might let you compete after all!"

"Oh. My. God!" Danica cried. She leaped into Haydee's arms, almost knocking the poor thing into the cave wall.

Haydee picked herself up, laughing. "Don't get too excited too soon. Simona said she's *thinking* about it—she said she'll meet with you tomorrow morning to discuss. But let me tell you: I put in a good word for you, and it's looking promising, I won't lie!"

"You did? You put in a good word for me?" Danica said. "Thank you so much!"

"Now, I can't take all the credit. Don't just thank me. Thank Cassie, too."

"Cassie?" Danica said in a dull voice.

She looked just as confused as Micah was.

"Just talk to Simona. And then if all goes well, meet me tomorrow for practice. Danica, you could win this contest!" Haydee said. And she was off. And Danica was left staring at the van that Cassie was in, a searing-cold look on her face.

"What did Cassie do?" Micah asked.

She wouldn't answer him, just shook her head. "I can't believe her," she said.

Nine

It was Tuesday at 8:59 A.M. and Danica was standing with Cassie outside Simona's office. This time, she took care to wear an actual pair of shorts instead of a bikini. She swore she still had scars left over from Simona's wicker couch.

Cassie hadn't said more than two words since they'd arrived to wait for their 9:00 A.M. appointment and Danica was sick of it. The problem with having enemies is that they don't like talking to you. *Everyone always wants to talk to me*, Danica thought. *And Cassie is not going to be the exception.*

Danica turned to Cassie, just as Cassie was turning to her.

"So—" they both said at the same time.

"Oh sorry," Cassie said.

"You talk," Danica said. "What were you going

to say?" She was ready to see the real side of Cassie, the Cassie that had made it pro and won contests and intimidated other surfers and was supposed to be so *good*, though Danica hadn't been witness to it. Where was that girl?

"I wanted to ask you a question," Cassie said.

"Then ask it."

Now that they were alone, Danica expected Cassie to throw down. To step up. To say something like, *If you're back in the surf contest, you'd better bring it.* Danica could picture this whole transaction so vividly: like another sequel to *Bring It On* but soaked in saltwater, Danica in the Kirsten Dunst/Hayden Panettiere role, obviously.

Except there was no bringing much of anything, because Cassie just said, "Are you and Micah back together?"

"Excuse me?" Danica said, caught off guard.

That's when Simona opened her office door. "Come in, C.I.T.s," she said.

Danica stepped in first, glad she didn't have to answer Cassie's question.

Simona sat them both down and started talking. "Haydee really pleaded your case, Danica. Apparently she thinks it's very important that you take part in the expo this weekend. What do you think about that?"

"I want to surf in the contest," Danica burst out. "I really want to." She didn't care how pathetic she might look begging like this in front of Cassie—it was the honest truth.

"I know you do," Simona said. "You'll be surfing against local Kona surfers and also campers from the Hilo Surfgirl camp across the island, did you know that?"

"Does that mean I'm back in the contest?"

"I didn't say that . . . yet. I just want you to understand that Camp Ohana needs to have its best face on for the expo. Our reputation is on the line. This contest is what determines who will compete in the inter-camp contest in Oahu and—"

Danica shot up in her chair, letting out a yelp before Simona could even finish. "I knew it!" she cried. "I knew the winners at the expo would get to go to Oahu! That's the top secret prize, isn't it?"

"Hush," Simona said, motioning for Danica to sit down. Danica did, trying to keep calm. Of note was the fact that Cassie had not uttered a single word about this exciting bit of news. She was just sitting there, staring at the wall. *Odd*, Danica thought.

"All this leaves me in a quandary," Simona continued, throwing up her hands. "And then of course there's the Cassie factor."

Danica snapped out of her excitement. "What about Cassie?"

"I can't punish only you, Danica, if there was another C.I.T. involved in sneaking off the property," Simona said. Her eyes settled on Cassie. "Cassie has admitted to it, haven't you, Cassie?"

Cassie nodded almost eagerly. What was her deal?

"And we can't imagine the surf contest without you in it, Cassie," Simona said. She turned to Danica, as if in an afterthought. "Without the both of you."

Oh. It's not that she needs me to surf, Danica realized, her stomach sinking. *It's that she needs Cassie. Everyone just assumes Cassie will be the one to win.*

Simona announced her decision: Danica would be allowed to compete in the surf contest this weekend after all, and Cassie would still be allowed to compete, too. But that didn't mean they were free from punishment. They were assigned to kitchen duty for the rest of the week. And they were both on warning. Next time, they could be kicked out.

"Wait, so I'm really still in the contest?" Cassie shot out before Simona could finish her sentence.

Danica looked at her in surprise. Did she—could it be?—sound disappointed?

"Yes, that's what I said," Simona said. "You expected to lose your spot, didn't you?"

"Yeah," Cassie said, staring at her hands. "I didn't think you'd let me surf. Because of . . . of what I did."

"Well, you got lucky today then, didn't you?"

Cassie mumbled something indecipherable, so Simona repeated herself. "Didn't you?"

Cassie finally looked up. "I guess so," she said. That's when it became clear to Danica: The girl was freaked out. Call it a shark, call it a fear of going up against Danica, whatever—she was scared to surf. She wanted an out, and she didn't get it.

Danica expected to be happy to have this information, but she wasn't. She didn't know why she wasn't. She put the knowledge aside and turned to Simona.

"Thank you, Simona," Danica said. "I really appreciate this second chance. You know all I wanted to do this weekend was compete."

"You're welcome, Danica," Simona said.

"Yeah, thanks, Simona," Cassie mumbled.

Outside Simona's office, the two girls walked back to the beach with a tense silence between them.

Cassie was the one to break it. "Kitchen duty, huh? How bad could it be?"

"Bad," Danica said. "Very bad. But it's worth it." Then she couldn't help but add, "I'm pumped for Saturday, aren't you?"

"Uh-huh," Cassie said unconvincingly. She was a terrible liar. "I'm glad you get to compete. Everyone should be able to."

"Yeah, but don't think it's going to be easy. I might just knock you out of the water."

Cassie shrugged. "You might," was all she said.

It really was no fun competing against someone who didn't want to be there. But Danica wasn't going to complain. She was obviously about to win it all. And, from the look on Cassie's face, the so-called pro surfer knew it, too.

I should have just admitted the truth, Cassie was thinking the next morning. Because, yes: Tori had been right. Tori was always right. Give Tori a medal for always knowing everything. Cassie had said all those things down in the lava tunnels on purpose . . . hoping Simona would hear. Only, it had sort of backfired.

Clearly, Cassie had expected to be banned from the contest. She'd wanted to be off the hook, for it to be no fault of her own that she couldn't surf on Saturday. Then the conquering-her-fears hokey milestone of the summer could wait until next week, or the week after. She could stretch it out over the whole summer. Maybe by August she'd be ready to hop back on the board. Maybe then.

Simona had called her lucky. Cassie felt just the opposite.

Fact is, Saturday was quickly approaching and if she didn't want to make a total fool of herself in front of everyone at camp then she had to deal with this right now.

That's why she was up so early in the morning.

It was time. She could do this.

She stood waist deep in the water, her yellow board floating idly at her side. She just stood there.

I can do this, she repeated to herself.

And the board at her side didn't say a word.

For a second, she almost wished she would run into Micah. He usually surfed this spot early mornings, didn't he? So where was he today? Really, she had no idea because it wasn't like they'd said two words to each other since the horror show over the weekend.

Plus—she remembered, her stomach sinking—it wasn't like he was into her. He liked Danica, obviously. By now, they were probably boyfriend-girlfriend (whatever that entailed) and off basking in the sun together or whatever. So, really, it was better for her sanity and her focus if she didn't run into Micah. Surfing with a fear of sharks was bad enough—she couldn't imagine what it would be like to surf with a broken heart.

Cassie shook her head of all thoughts related to Micah and gazed out at the stretch of ocean before her. She didn't know if anything was more beautiful than this patch of Kona water in the early morning sunlight. She loved this place. She loved this water. That was the truth.

As she waded farther in, she heard Tori's voice shouting her name. "Wait up!"

Tori ran up, dragging one of the camp's white surfboards behind her. She dove into the water and paddled with loud splashes over to where Cassie stood in the water.

"Can I join you?" Tori said. That was the thing about Tori. No matter what she found out about her cousin, no matter how flawed Cassie turned out to be, Tori was always there by her side. Accepting her for her. Now *that* was what made Cassie lucky.

"What are you even doing up, Tor?" Cassie said. "What time is it?"

"Insane o'clock in the morning, what else! I thought I'd hang with you since you spend, like, all your free time doing dishes now. I never get to see you!"

"I know, it sucks," Cassie said.

"So . . ." Tori said, pausing meaningfully. "We're going surfing today, huh?"

"*We?*" Cassie said with amusement.

"What, don't you think I'm dressed for it?" Tori

did a quick turn to model her cute polka-dot bikini.

"You look great," Cassie said. "You're all spotty."

Tori smiled. The waves were building, starting to crash around them. Cassie was feeling the momentum. She felt the salt spray on the wind, the warm jostle of the currents under the water. She got up on the board, straddled it. She was here with her cousin Tori and for some reason that made her feel totally safe.

"You can do it," Tori said, eyes solemn in the bright sunlight. "I know it, Cass. I *know*."

Hearing Tori say it, seeing her eyes—it sort of made Cassie believe it, too.

"I'm gonna try," she said. She put a hand over her own eyes and gazed out at the rolling waves. "I'll try for one of those."

"You go!" Tori said. "I'll hang here." She stretched out full-length on her board like a sunbather. As Cassie paddled toward the bigger waves she saw Tori lift an arm in the air and give her a thumbs-up.

Cassie was paddling. She was moving faster, faster. A nice wave was coming at her and she was going to jump up to meet it.

She heard Tori yelling: "Go! Go! Go!"

She heard the wind rushing in her ears, the water splashing.

She saw the wave coming.

And then she saw it go. The wave went far, far away into the distance—a beautiful sight to see, except Cassie wasn't riding on it. Cassie was right where she was, immobile.

Soon, Tori paddled over on her board. Cassie knew she was about to give some encouragement, attempt to get her pumped up to try again, no matter how many tries it took. But then, without Cassie having to say a word, Tori seemed to sense something and her expression shifted. "We can just lounge on the boards . . ." she said gently. "It's too early to get a real tan, but we can try . . ."

Cassie shrugged. She wanted to cry, but she didn't. "We can do that just as well on the sand, can't we?" she choked out.

"Sure," Tori said. "Let's totally hit the sand. We have time before breakfast. And I have magazines in my bag and everything."

Gratefully, Cassie followed her cousin out of the ocean. She wasn't sure how she'd make it through the expo on Saturday. She had a sinking feeling she knew just what would happen if she bailed out on everyone and didn't surf, and it would have nothing to do with garbage duty or a few more sinks of dirty dishes.

If she didn't surf the expo, she'd lose her spot at Ohana. They'd send her home.

Ten

Cassie was set to surf in the first heat. There she was, the morning of the expo, dressed in her bikini and her rash guard, waxing her board on the sand—just like any other surfer prepping to compete. Still, she hadn't practiced first; she couldn't. She hadn't actually taken one solid ride on her surfboard since the accident . . . the incident . . . the . . . there was no word for it. Just call it the day that effectively sunk her whole entire life.

But if I don't surf, I'll get kicked out of Ohana, Cassie told herself. *If I don't have Ohana, what do I have . . . ? I have to surf today. I have to.*

Telling herself this didn't make it any easier. She could hardly keep her head on straight, and the self-imposed guilt trip wasn't helping.

Besides, there was the noise. Lots of it. The

people, everywhere. The campers chanting and cheering—maybe even for her. The announcers pumping up the crowd over the speakers; the ocean cleared, ready for the show; the colorful flags whipping in the wind. There was Danica, stretching out on her own board, set to surf a later heat. And there was Micah, hanging out with the guys. The boys' heats would come later. It was undeniable: Today was the expo and Cassie was going to have to take part in it, or else.

She remembered the competitions she'd been in over the years. What she usually felt when she was about to show her stuff in a surf contest was an exhilarated high, her heart pounding steadily, her focus studied and sharp. Surfing or not surfing was never the question—winning was. At least that's how it used to be.

Now there was no time for the inner psychobabble that might conquer her fears. She was set to go in the very first heat. This was round one of the girls' contest, with Camp Ohana surfers pitted against local teenagers from Kona and against surfers from another summer camp on Big Island called Hilo Surfgirls. The surfers who won their heats in this first round went on to round two. Then the surfers in round two went against one another to determine the ultimate winner. After the afternoon's expo events, points would be tallied and the winners and prize would be announced. Even so, Cassie didn't want to make it to round two. She just wanted to get through this one heat, this one round. Surf a couple runs, hold her head up, let someone else get the win for a change.

How hard could that be?

The surfers for the first heat were lining up now. Cassie took her spot beside the two girls she was competing against this round. The whistle blew. And they were off!

Cassie lifted her surfboard over her head and ran for the water. The girl in the red suit was from Kona; she reached the water first. The girl in the black suit was from the Hilo Surfgirls camp; she was going pro, that's the talk Cassie had heard on the beach. They both seemed like strong competitors. *Good*, Cassie thought. *Maybe one of them will be awesome. Maybe one will be so good, she'll dominate the whole heat and won't give anyone else a shot at a wave.* A girl could hope, anyway.

Soon enough, the three competitors were paddling out toward deeper water. Whoever rode the most waves successfully won the heat. These were simpler rules than Cassie was used to—she was fine with that.

The Kona girl took the first wave—she sailed far and fast, and the crowd cheered. The Hilo Surfgirls camper caught a wave, bigger than the first, and wowed the crowd with a perfect cutback. Cassie, for her part, hadn't gone for a wave yet. Now the Kona girl was paddling back, ready for a second wave. When one came, Cassie let her have it.

Cassie thought she heard someone yelling her name, but she didn't turn toward shore to see who it was. Her breathing was fast, her limbs heavy, her grip on the board loose and not steady at all.

The Hilo Surfgirls camper paddled closer. "What's up?" she called over to Cassie. "Taking your time? The heat's over in, like, three minutes."

Cassie shrugged. "I'm just waiting for the right wave," she called back.

The other girl pointed out in the distance. "That one looks just right," she yelled. "Race ya for it!" She started paddling. Cassie found herself caught up in the moment. She started going for it, too. Then she realized what she was doing and she reacted fast. She was turning her board, turning in a whole other direction. She was still paddling, and faster than before, but not toward that wave and not toward any other wave. She was paddling in the only direction she could. She was paddling back in.

Minutes later, Cassie stood dripping onshore. She'd let go of her yellow surfboard and it lay flat at her feet, still attached to her ankle by its leash. Voices seemed to be coming at her from every direction.

"What *was* that out there?" a C.I.T. was saying.

"She choked!" said another. "Did you see her choke?!"

"She did not just leave in the middle of a heat. She has to be joking. Please tell me she's joking," Haydee, one of the surf counselors, said.

"Dude, I don't think she's joking," Zeke, the other surf counselor, said.

"Giving the heat to those other girls would be

the lamest joke ever," Danica said. "Cassie, if you didn't want to surf, why didn't you just say so?"

"Yeah, Cassie, why?" said someone else.

"Are you okay?" Andi said, pushing through the crowd. Tori was behind her and repeated it: "Omigod, are you okay? Are you okay?"

"Cassie, I don't understand what just happened. What's the problem?" Simona asked. She stepped through everyone else and stood right in front of Cassie, wanting a response.

It was all too much. Maybe Cassie could have had a clear and coherent answer, if they all weren't ganging up on her like this. Across the sand, the whistle went off. Cassie's heat was over and she didn't even get a place in it; she was disqualified. Now she was going home for sure. They might as well point her to the bunk and send her packing.

She opened her mouth to explain, but what came out was just, "I'm sorry, I wasn't ready, I tried, I—" She saw Micah on the edge of the crowd, saw him eyeing her, seeming like he wanted to say something but not. After the show she just put on, he'd probably never speak to her again. There was only one word for how she felt: ashamed.

Defeated, she bent down and unhooked the leash from her ankle. Her surfboard lay unattached, facedown on the wet sand.

Simona put her arm around Cassie and led her away. Cassie was reeling. It was all happening so fast—going to camp, being a normal kid, getting kicked out. Did it even happen? She felt numb as she followed Simona to a stand of palm trees on the edge of the beach.

"Your coach called and told me about your accident," Simona said softly, once they were alone. "I didn't realize it was still such an issue."

Cassie changed the subject. "Can I stay the night?" she asked. "Can I watch the rest of the expo and see who wins the surf contest and hang out with my cousin a little and just stay the one night?"

Simona stared at Cassie, confused. "What are you talking about?"

Cassie tried to pull herself together. She was a pro surfer, and if a pro ran out of the ocean like she just did in a real contest? Why, she'd surely lose her sponsor and her spot on the team. "I'm talking about getting kicked out of camp," Cassie told Simona calmly. She felt sure she knew the consequences.

"Cassie." Simona had her hands on both of Cassie's shoulders, like she wanted to shake her. "I never said anything about you being kicked out."

"But I choked," Cassie said. "Didn't you see me choke?"

"I saw," Simona said.

"And?" Cassie said. Now she was the one who was confused. *Aren't they going to send me home?* she thought.

Simona cleared her throat. Cassie expected a speech. Something about courage and overcoming fear and how nothing happened with that shark and she needed to face it and get on with her life. All speeches she'd heard before—from her coach, from her parents, from everyone, pretty much, except Tori.

But all Simona said was, "Cassie, are you all right?"

"I—" Cassie started to say that of course she was all right; she was always all right. But in reality she wasn't. Maybe it was time to tell an adult.

"No," she admitted. "I couldn't surf today, I just couldn't. I have to be perfect or else there's no point doing it at all."

"Cassie, I understand, I do. But you have to understand something as well—this is camp, not the pro circuit. You don't have to be perfect. I'm sorry if the surfing contest made you think that, but we just want you to have fun, that's what this is about. It's the summer. You're a C.I.T. You're sixteen! It's time to relax and have fun."

Cassie gazed down at her toes. While Simona had been talking she'd gone ahead and buried them in the sand. That's about how she felt, covered up and barely able to breathe. It would be nice to give up and relax, to allow herself to simply have fun for once in her life. "I don't know how to do that," Cassie admitted.

"Don't you worry," Simona said. "I'll keep my eye on you. We'll work at it."

"Okay," Cassie said. "Is it true about Oahu?" she added. "Do the winners of this contest get to go?"

Simona smiled, zipped her lips, and didn't say a word.

Cassie was beginning to realize just how big this Oahu contest was supposed to be, and she could have been in it. *But you know what? Maybe it's not my contest to win*, she thought.

She noticed Danica standing on the sand, stretching before her bright pink board, a determined look on her face. Her heat was up next. Danica saw Cassie and shook her head. Then, uncharacteristically, she gave a slight smile. *Next time*, she mouthed.

Cassie nodded, acknowledging the dare. *Next time*, she thought. Next time, in fact, she had a feeling Danica might be the one to beat.

Then Cassie set her eyes on someone else. Someone she'd been avoiding all week and would probably avoid for the rest of her life, thanks to what just happened.

There he was, Micah. He was standing beside his surfboard, looking out toward the water. He had this intense look on his face, completely focused— Cassie knew it well. She also had a feeling he had a good shot at the prize. But she didn't walk over and tell him that. She just watched him for a long moment until he turned and she was afraid he'd see. Then she looked away.

"I'm going to get a good spot on the beach," Cassie told Simona, finally beginning to relax a little. "You know . . . to see who wins."

Danica nailed her first heat, and then her second. She was a clear choice for the winner, once the points were tallied. Cassie sat back and watched, not exactly surprised. Okay, maybe a little. Danica had talked the talk, but Cassie wasn't sure if she'd be able to live up to it. And here she did.

Tori came up and put her arm around Cassie. "You sure you're okay?" she asked Cassie.

"I'm better than I was this morning," Cassie admitted. It was true: Though she felt mortified, she also felt honest. She'd finally done what *she* wanted to do, not what anyone else wanted. It was freeing.

Together, Tori and Cassie watched Danica walk across the patch of sand like she owned it.

"I'll hate her if you want me to," Tori said.

"Nah," Cassie said. "No need."

"Are you sure about that?" Tori said. Danica and Micah were now at the shoreline, talking.

Cassie looked, then stopped looking, then stopped trying to seem like she wasn't looking and just openly watched them. Micah was patting Danica on the shoulder in congratulations for a good show at the contest. Danica was pulling him in for a hug. Then they were hugging—out there, in the bright sun, for anyone to see. It pained Cassie to watch it, but she couldn't help it.

Tori raised an eyebrow. "Did he talk to you about what happened?" she asked.

"He who?"

Tori set her eyes on Cassie like she was dumb. Of course *he* was Micah.

Cassie let out a huge sigh. "Not yet."

A whistle blew. It was the guys' turn at the surf contest now. Micah was in the first heat. Cassie watched him line up, run into the water with his two competitors, and paddle out for the waves. She had a feeling about him—a feeling he'd win.

"Maybe he's waiting for me to talk to him first," Cassie said. "And Tori? The answer to the question I know you want to ask me is yes. I like him, okay? I *like* him. It's way too late, obviously. But now you know."

Strangely, Tori started to smile, a smile so wide it showed teeth. "Good," she said. "Because I happened upon some information that just might interest you . . ."

"What information?"

"Danica and Micah? Not an item."

Cassie whipped around to stare at her cousin. "Really?"

"I wouldn't lie about that," Tori said. "Pinkie swear."

"So . . ." Cassie said.

Tori continued to smile impassively.

"So now that you told me, aren't you going to say anything else?" Cassie said. "Like, tell me what I should do about it?"

Tori turned to her, serious now. "Are you asking me for advice?"

"You're the one with the boyfriend . . ." Cassie said.

Tori shrugged. "Who knows how long that'll last."

"What is *that* supposed to mean?"

Tori shook her head quickly. "Nothing," she said. "Eddie and me, we don't have much to talk about—he's a little boring, if you want the truth." She changed the subject. "But you know what? If you want Micah to know you like him, you have to do this really insane thing I've only heard about.

It's, like, totally intense. I don't know if I should tell you . . ."

"Tell me," Cassie insisted. She could see that the first of the guys had taken a wave. The crowd was getting on their feet now, cheering and yelling. Over the noise, Cassie said, "Tor, you have to tell me."

They stood up together, toes in the sand. Tori had a crazy-serious look on her face. "I don't know, Cass. I don't know if you could handle it."

"I can handle it!" Cassie protested.

Tori was shaking her head, but she finally relented. "Fine, I'll tell you—but only because you're my flesh and blood." She paused, taking a breath. Micah was paddling out for a wave now. Cassie's focus was split—half on Micah, half on the wisdom Tori was about to impart to her. It was some L.A. thing, probably. Something the celebrities did instead of normal flirting. Still, Cassie was dying to know what it was.

"Are you ready?" Tori said.

Cassie nodded solemnly.

"Okay, when he's done with this contest you go over to him. You tap him on the shoulder. He turns around. You open your mouth, and"—Tori paused, drawing it out—"you tell him you like him."

Cassie shook her head in confusion. "That's it?"

Tori burst out laughing. "Yeah, what did you think I was gonna say? Bite him like a vampire?"

Cassie shook her head at Tori's ridiculousness. She should have known it was all a joke. Then she watched Micah catch his first wave. And his next. She watched him surf with the passion she used to have. It made her like him even more, seeing that in him. And when he was clearly the winner of his heat, she felt truly happy for him. Just beamingly happy. Like, even if she followed Tori's advice and walked up to him and tapped him on the shoulder and burst out with the fact that she was a dope and sorry-sorry-sorry, oh, and btw, I, like, totally like you and he laughed in her face and said he wasn't interested, even then?

Even then she'd still be happy for him. He deserved it.

The rest of the water-sports expo was—shockingly—a blast. Cassie found herself able to relax, and even Tori began to get into it (though she still had her swimming levels to conquer; Cassie reminded herself to deal with that next week). Cassie even saw that little camper Abby try an event in the expo—she skidded belly down on her wakeboard for a long minute, laughing the whole time. She definitely seemed more comfortable in the water. Cassie also saw other C.I.T.s and junior counselors and counselors she knew taking part in the expo, everyone seeming to be having so much fun, like that was the point of the whole thing in the first place. Huh. Maybe it was.

Then it was time for the winners of the surf contest to be officially announced. Cassie had predicted the outcome exactly: Danica snagged the top prize for the girls' contest, and Micah the boys'. Cassie and the other C.I.T.s crowded around the winners as the prize was finally revealed. Cassie found herself beside Andi, who had taken part in three events in the expo—windsurfing, wakeboarding, and surfing. "You did great," Cassie said. "I was watching you out there."

"It was fun," Andi said. "But you—" She paused awkwardly. "When you're ready to surf again, I know you'll rock."

"Thanks, Andi," Cassie said quietly. She was about to say something else, like she hoped Andi wouldn't think any less of her now, because she was really hoping they could be friends, but before she could get the words out Simona made the grand announcement everyone had been waiting for:

Danica and Micah, as the two winners, would be representing Camp Ohana in the inter-camp surfing competition in Oahu! The contest was sooner than anyone realized—they'd be leaving in just a few days for an overnight trip to Oahu island.

"That is so not fair!" Andi shrieked. "I bet they're putting them up in a superfancy hotel. Do you know how much I miss real sheets?"

Cassie didn't get a chance to respond. Tori was running up, her cheeks flushed. Cassie just assumed she was excited. She grabbed Cassie's hand and held it. "Ohmygod areyouokay?" Tori said in a rush.

"Yeah," Cassie said. "Why?"

Tori's eyes were bugging out of her head. "What do you mean?" she hissed. She pulled Cassie away. "Cass," she continued, "they're going away together—to a *hotel*."

Cassie nodded. Then it hit her. It just *hit*. She

had to tell Micah she had feelings for him very, very soon—if he and Danica weren't already back together, they surely would be by the end of this trip. She had to say something now, or it would be too late.

Eleven

Danica was packing for Oahu and Sierra and Sasha were helping her, as usual. Actually, Danica was just lounging on her bed in the C.I.T. bunk while they were doing all the work sorting through her clothes and swimsuits, holding up options for her to say yea or nay to. She was supposed to be ready to catch the hopper plane in about an hour.

"Sure," she said in approval to the emerald green Three Dots tank top Sierra held up.

"No way, are you an idiot?" she said to a mustard-yellow American Apparel T-shirt dress that was so last summer she had no clue how it had slipped into her suitcase in the first place.

"Sorry," Sasha said quickly. She kicked the offending item under her bed.

"So," Sierra said loudly, "you think you and

217

Micah will get to hang out alone at the hotel?"

"Of course not!" Danica said. "You know the counselors are going to be chaperoning us the whole time! They'd never let us go otherwise. I'm sharing a room with Haydee."

Sasha wrinkled her nose. "That sucks," she said. "How are you gonna get him alone with Haydee watching all the time? Bummer."

"Well, there's always Zeke," Sierra said. "He lives on another planet . . . he won't notice anything. So just sneak off to Micah's room."

"True," Sasha said. "Right, Danica?"

Right, Danica thought. But she didn't say it out loud.

Actually, she wanted Sasha and Sierra to lower their voices—Cassie was across the bunk on her bed with her cousin, Tori. After the weird are-you-into-Micah moment outside Simona's office, Danica wanted to keep her Micah plans on the down-low, at least until she landed at the hotel suite and figured out a way to get his attention.

Cassie had obviously caught wind of the conversation because she was looking over. But she stayed in place on her bed, a coward.

No wait. Something else is going on. It had taken Danica a while, but she just noticed that second how Cassie and Tori weren't sitting on the other side of the bunk chatting about the usual boring junk that made Danica's eyes water. No, in fact, it looked like Tori was crying, and Cassie was now pulling her in for a hug.

Danica sat up. "What happened?" she called across the bunk toward Tori and Cassie. "Tori, you're not *that* upset your cousin made a total fool of herself at the expo, are you?"

Tori and Cassie both looked at her in surprise. Tori was actually crying—she had streaks of tears all down her face. *Trés* unflattering. Cassie's face darkened for a moment, but she held in any response.

"That's not why I'm upset," Tori said. "It's Eddie."

"Eddie who?" Danica said.

"Eddie," Cassie said, like now Danica was the idiot. "Her boyfriend."

"Oh," Danica breathed. "He dumped you." Normally she'd be all interested in the dirt, but this was camper dirt, not C.I.T. or counselor dirt, so naturally it was not interesting enough to get up off the bed and go over and ask for details. Tori was only fourteen, after all—a baby. Whoever this Eddie kid was, surely Danica wouldn't care one way or the other if he was single.

"He didn't dump her," Cassie said. "Actually, like I was saying, Tor, you said you guys didn't have much to talk about, that he was boring, right? So it's better this way."

Tori nodded. "It is," she agreed. "It was totally mutual," she added through a honk and a sniffle into a wad of tissues.

Now this is getting disgusting, Danica thought. "Then why are you crying?" she said, beyond perplexed. When she'd let go of Micah at the end of last summer it had been like a shrug, like, *See ya! Wouldn't want to be ya!*

In hindsight, that had been a huge mistake. But she hadn't cried then, and she wasn't crying now. Thankfully, she was going on this trip away to Oahu where she would have a chance to fix it. Losing interest in Tori's so-called love life, she turned back to Sierra and Sasha, who were always rapt in attention whenever she wanted (or pretended to want) their advice.

"What outfit do you think will help me get Micah back?" she said. "The Lacoste or the Calvin Klein?" She said it like she was sure of the outcome, no matter the outfit, but in fact she wasn't too sure. Not sure at all.

Sierra and Sasha couldn't decide. "They're both good," Sierra said.

"Either way, he'll take you back for sure," Sasha said.

"Like, totally for sure," Sierra added.

I hope so, Danica thought but didn't say.

Instead, she stood up all confidently and held the Lacoste outfit against her body, checking herself out in the mirror. In the reflection she caught sight of Cassie—she'd gotten off her bed, slipped on her flip-flops, and was flying out the door. Like she suddenly decided she had something to do.

But what? Danica thought. She turned and found Tori still on Cassie's bed, still feeling sorry for herself, obviously. But she'd stopped crying at least. She looked like she knew something Danica didn't.

"Where'd Cassie just go?" Danica called over to Tori.

"Out," Tori said.

Danica didn't trust her one bit. "For what?" she said.

Tori stretched out on Cassie's bed, just making herself at home in the bunk like she was a C.I.T. and not a camper. Danica made a mental note to put the kid in her place when she returned from Oahu. "I'm thirsty," Tori said. "Cassie went to get me something to drink." She sat up then, her eyes hard and fast on Danica. "I'm dying for a soda."

Cassie was not headed to the canteen for a soda. She was on her way across the sand to the *humuhumunukunukuapua'a* bunk—to look for Micah.

Hearing Danica say that she was going to try to get Micah back gave her a jolt of motivation. She was full of courage, all ready to get it out in the open. Tori had said that if she liked Micah, she should just tell him, and that's what she was going to do. Tell him.

It sounded simple—but witnessing Tori all broken up over what happened between her and Eddie (though she kept saying it had been 100 percent mutual and no big), Cassie wondered if having a boyfriend was truly worth it.

What if it doesn't work out? she thought. Fact is, it might not work out. Micah could laugh in her face. He could tell her she was a snob and he had no interest in her. He could say he wanted to be with a *real* surfer, not a girl who went around saying she was pro but couldn't even stand up on her own two feet on her board. He could say he liked Danica. He could say any number of things—the possibilities were endless, and endlessly frightening.

And what if he said what she wanted him to say? What if he said he liked her, too, what then?

They could get together and be having the time of their lives and then out of nowhere, something could go sour between them, something uncontrollable, something that made no sense. And *then* what?

Then it would hurt like nothing Cassie had ever experienced before. She wouldn't know what to do. What if that happened? What if, what if.

Just as she stood there, on the lanai of the *humuhumunukunukuapua'a* bunk, about to knock and see if she could come in, the door opened. And he was on the other side, facing her, just inches

223

away. He was carrying a duffel bag—obviously ready to leave for his trip.

"Hey," she said.

"Hey," he said.

Her stomach dropped. He was still mad at her over how bratty she'd acted at the beach. He had every right to be mad. She'd never explained. She never even said she was sorry. Or, worse, he didn't even want to be seen with her after witnessing her run out on the surfing contest. Who would?!

She was thinking, *This is it. He says hey, I say hey, and he leaves on his trip and I never tell him the truth and I regret it forever and ever.*

But before she could wallow in this, he surprised her. He smiled, the smile that sent her stomach leaping till she felt like she would tip over. "I think you've got the wrong bunk," he said. "This is *B*-16, not G-16. Don't you see the door?" He pointed at the peeling, barely readable B-16 painted on the bunk's door.

She laughed, and smiled back. "No, I'm not lost," she said. "Think we could talk for a second? There's some stuff I want to say."

Micah led Cassie to the stand of hammocks between the two C.I.T. bunks. Usually, on a Sunday, the C.I.T.s' day off, someone was lying in one of them, trying to escape from the chaos that was Ohana, but Micah and Cassie had come at a good moment. They were alone.

"Congratulations," Cassie burst out. "You were intense out there. I was impressed."

"Yeah?" he said, trying to keep all expression off his face. Truth is he'd wanted to impress her. He'd wanted her to see he was serious about surfing, serious like she was. It was stupid, he knew, to care what a girl thought, but he did.

"Definitely," she said. She sat in one of the hammocks, swinging there idly. A few long seconds passed between them. "Definitely," she repeated.

That's all she wanted to tell me, he realized. He was embarrassed to admit to himself that he'd thought it might be something else.

"I'm sorry you weren't ready to surf," he said. "But, you know, you're ready when you're ready." This was coming out all mangled. He tried again. "I mean, everyone gets it. *I* get it." What he wanted her to know was that he was there for her, if she ever felt like talking about it, but she was making him nervous and he decided to stop talking.

She seemed to catch his good intentions, though, because her cheeks flushed a little and she said, "Thanks."

"Sure," he said.

The awkward silence expanded, making it impossible for him to say anything else. He figured he should just get up to go. The van was waiting . . .

Then Cassie spoke again, and this time in a rush. "I also wanted to say I'm sorry. I'm so, so sorry for how I acted at the beach last week, how awful I was, and I was just scared, you know? I was just scared and I didn't want to tell you. I mean, *obviously* I was scared—look at what happened—and maybe if I talked to you about it first, I, oh I don't know."

"I know," he said. He was looking into her eyes, these huge blue eyes, the kind of blue you'd expect her to have, the color of the water. He was having a problem looking away from those eyes. "I'm not mad," he added. "I was just confused."

"About what?" she said.

Now he sat in one of the hammocks. He needed something to do with himself while he talked, so he kicked off and started swinging. "About what was going on, you know, between us."

Her blue eyes were locked with his, even as he kept swinging.

"*If* there was anything going on between us," he added lamely.

She spoke up. "I think maybe there was," she said. "I was hoping there was."

"You were?"

"I was wondering, like, *Is this a date?* That's what I kept thinking, but—" She bowed her head, her cheeks flaming up.

"Stupid idea for a date," he said. "I'm sorry."

"Wait, *was* it a date?" she asked in a low voice.

They were too far away to have this conversation. He got up off his hammock and crossed the swath of sand to hers. He sat beside her and as he did the hammock sunk down toward the ground, but still it held the both of them. "I thought it was," he said.

She just smiled.

"Was that the right answer?" he said.

"Yeah," she said. "Most definitely yeah."

Then they sat there, close together, not saying

anything for the longest time. Micah didn't want to break the silence this time, though he knew he had to get to the van soon to catch the ride to the airport. Still, he reached out his arm and put it around her. She looked at him, and he looked at her, and—you know what?—he was about to have his dreams come true and compete in a real surfing contest, but all he wanted was to sit here with Cassie a little longer before that happened. He didn't want to leave.

Cassie was at the van, saying good-bye to Micah. He'd be away only two nights. Two nights, that's it! They could talk about whatever mysterious something was happening between them when he got back. She could handle two nights of not-knowing-for-sure. Two nights were nothing.

He stowed his duffel bag and surfboard in the back of the van and jumped down.

"So," he said.

"So," she replied. She was always repeating whatever he said back to him.

There were too many people around to have

a real conversation, so she figured they'd leave it at that.

Then he shocked her by leaning down toward her. His face was getting closer and closer to hers—like, seriously, six inches away, then four, then two, then his lips were about to land on hers. This was the moment when he'd kiss her, out here in the open where anybody walking by could see. She was so sure it was happening, really and truly happening, that she closed her eyes and just let it happen.

It would be bliss.

Except not.

The kiss-to-be never ended up catching her. Someone had called his name, and the face that had almost been up close and personal with hers never got there. Cassie opened her eyes and saw Danica running up. "Can you help me with my board?" she called to Micah.

"Uh, yeah," he said awkwardly, and went to her.

Cassie stood there, dazed. *Did anyone see that he was about to kiss me?* she thought. *I hope I didn't imagine it.*

But after everyone said their good-byes and

Micah and Danica and the surf counselors and junior counselors who were escorting them on the trip all got in the van to leave, Cassie was dead sure she had not been making it up. Micah waved, but that wasn't what convinced her. It was the look on Danica's face. Cold. Hard. Ready to kill.

Cassie was frozen in place as the van pulled out of the parking lot and into the road. What a way to ruin a moment.

"Cass!" the sound of a familiar voice shouting out her name derailed her train of thought. Cassie turned to find Tori and some of her *pinao* bunkmates running up in bathing suits, trailing towels. "You're the swimming C.I.T. Come chaperone us! Please, please!"

Tori had just been sobbing into Cassie's arms over some unworthy boy and now it looked like she was back to her old self—and even voluntarily wanting to swim! *She sure got over that one fast*, Cassie thought. *How does she do it?*

Then there was no time to dwell over anything—not how quickly Tori could bounce back, not the drama Cassie would surely face once Danica returned, not the fact that Cassie still hadn't managed to get back on her surfboard, and not even what was happening with Micah. It was time to swim, and Cassie needed to grab a beach towel. The ocean was calling.

CHECK OUT A SNEAK PREVIEW OF

Summer SUNSET
CONFIDENTIAL

One

Cassie felt as if she were surfing. But she knew she wasn't. In fact, when she looked down she could see her white flip-flops trudging over the sand, and she could hear them click-clacking against her heels—but it didn't *feel* like she was walking at all. It was like the earth was moving beneath her and she was somehow managing to remain upright. As if she were gliding.

There's nothing like kissing the boy you're crazy about to make you lose all sensation in your legs.

Of course, she and Micah hadn't actually *kissed* kissed. They almost kissed. She'd puckered up, closed her eyes, and felt the warmth of his breath. But just before their lips came together, they were interrupted. By Danica of all people.

As disappointed as she was, Cassie had to

admit to the teensiest amount of relief, too. She hadn't been prepared for the kiss to happen, and she would have appreciated a little heads-up. Because the total lame reality of the situation was this: She really didn't have much experience in the whole making-out department.

What if she was bad at it? What if Micah *had* locked lips with her and then discovered she was terrible at it?

She did a quick mental recap: Micah liked her, and that was good. He wanted to kiss her, also good. But she had zero history with boyfriends and hardly any kissing experience (just party games and pecks on the cheek from friends). And that was bad. Sad, scary bad.

Micah, she knew, had had girlfriends. Maybe even lots of them. Including Danica, the smokin' hot alpha female of Camp Ohana. And—oh right! They just left together for the inter-camp surf competition in Oahu, where they would spend two nights in a hotel.

More bad.

Of course they had separate rooms and chaperones, but it didn't take Einstein to figure out that hotel plus ex-girlfriend plus honeymoon capital of the world equaled big reason to worry.

Cassie came to a stop. Now the light, gliding sensation was totally gone. Instead she could feel the unmistakable crashing, flailing, and total disorientation that came with a major wipeout.

It was almost like her shark attack all over again—the one bad experience that haunted her so much, she still couldn't bear to surf in deep water. Only instead of a Great White taking a chomp out of her board, it was her own daydreams getting munched in front of her.

Great. She'd had her first boyfriend for all of ten minutes and already she was stumped on what to do. There had to be something seriously wrong with her.

"Cass-*eeeeeeeee!*" a familiar female voice sang out her name.

Cassie turned and spotted her cousin, Tori, bounding toward her as fast as her high-heeled wedge sandals would allow.

How does she do it? Cassie wondered. Somehow, Tori always seemed to be wearing a brand-new outfit. But how was that even possible since campers were only allowed one trunk? Did she have a secret closet in the jungle? Did she have a magic passageway to Barneys?

"Okay, so . . . ?" Tori planted herself right in front of Cassie and started making little circular motions with her right hand—the one with the perfect pink-polished manicure.

That was something else about Tori. In addition to her enormous invisible closet, the girl seemed to have discovered a salon somewhere among the banyan trees.

"What?" Cassie replied.

Tori made a huffing noise and put her hands on her hips. "So did he kiss you?"

"Yeah. I mean . . . no. Not really."

"What does *that* mean?"

"We were just about to when we had to stop."

Her cousin frowned. "But he was coming in for an actual kiss, right? He wasn't trying to whisper in your ear or something?"

Cassie thought for a moment. No, they had definitely been in pre-make-out formation. His mouth had been heading for her mouth, not her ear. She knew what close whispering felt like and this was very different. This had been softer. Warmer. Tingly-er.

"It was a kiss. Or almost was, anyway."

Tori let out such a high-pitched squeal, Cassie fully expected a pack of dogs to come running up. "I'm so proud of you!" she gushed. She hooked her right arm around Cassie's left and started pulling her, half skipping, along the beach.

"Yeah, well. Don't congratulate me too soon," Cassie muttered. "Like I said, it wasn't technically a kiss."

"*Yet*," Tori stressed, still smiling smugly.

"And he's in Waikiki for a couple of days."

"Big deal."

"With his ex-girlfriend."

Tori's grin vanished. "Okay. That's pretty bad. I'll give you that."

Cassie sighed. She liked bubbly Tori better.

"But so what?" Tori asked. "He's had all this time to hook back up with Danica and he hasn't, right?"

"I guess not."

"That means it's really truly totally over. You know. Like when you can't even remember why you were into them in the first place."

"Uh, remember Tor. I've never had a boyfriend."

"Yeah, I know. But I meant guys you go out with."

"Had none of those either."

"Come on!" She bumped her shoulder against Cassie's. "You've had dates . . . Right?"

Cassie shook her head.

"Seriously? Not even, like, a just-for-prom boyfriend?"

"Nada."

"Okay, fine. But what about all those superhot surfer guys you travel with? You've at least started up something with one of them once upon a time? Right?"

Cassie shrugged. "I held hands with one or two while we walked on the beach."

Tori blinked back at her. "You held hands? That's it?"

"Why? What's wrong?"

"Nothing. That's . . . sweet. Really." Tori's smile seemed to freeze in place until it looked more like a wince. "It's just . . . I always assumed you'd had at least one or two flings. I thought it was, like, one of the perks of your job."

"What are you talking about? That would be

stupid. They're either my teammates or they're with my competitors. It would be so . . . wrong."

They walked in silence for a moment. Suddenly Tori came to a dead halt and gasped.

"What?" Cassie instinctively searched the waves for shark fins.

"*Shhh!*" Tori pulled her behind a bush. "Over there. It's Eddie. He's with Larkin Fennell. Can you believe it?"

"Um . . . I . . . guess not." Cassie took a moment to brace herself for the scorn of her cousin/executive social director. "Who's Larkin Fennell?"

Like clockwork, Tori's mouth dropped. She stared at Cassie as if she were turning mint green before her eyes. "She's the snootiest camper in this place. Where have you been?"

Cassie looked over at the girl. Olive-skinned with shiny brown hair cut in a bob. "She's pretty."

Tori made a snorting noise. "Best looks money can buy. Do you know she actually had a butler or something carry all her stuff to her bunkhouse? What a snot."

Cassie frowned. "Why do you care who he hangs out with, anyway? He's your ex. I thought you were over Eddie."

Again her cousin stared at her in disbelief—with a little pity thrown in. "You don't get it, do you?"

"No. Explain it."

"It's complicated—the whole deal with exes. It's never totally over. You don't want them back, exactly. But you don't want them to be all happy and hooked up with someone else."

Cassie waited. "And this is *why*?" she prompted.

"Because. It just is."

"So *not* what I needed to hear right now," Cassie grumbled, thinking of Micah and Danica.

Tori's eyes widened in minor horror. "Nananananananoh! That's so not going to happen with Micah. Like I said, their relationship has totally cooled off."

"I hope so," Cassie mumbled, flicking a bug off her arm. "I really hope so."